BEWARE THE POTUS

William I. Brazley Jr.

Enhanced
DNA
DEVELOP. NURTURE. ACHIEVE.
Publishing Division

BEWARE THE POTUS

Library of Congress Control Number: 2020919317
ISBN: 978-1-7351349-7-0

CHAPTER ONE

Crouching between two buildings, Colonel Dale Patton and his men tried to stay out of the moonlight. Their clothes were ringing wet as the desert heat made them sweat profusely. Their military fatigues challenged every move they made. Eyes, stinging from sweat, were red and swollen. What had been a platoon of six was now only four. Patton peeked around the corner of the building, looking for an escape vehicle. There was a truck about fifty yards down the street. That was forty yards too far. With the prisoner lying at his feet, Patton's most experienced officer checked his watch.

Captain Bobby Parker spoke with a hint of haste in his voice saying, "We've got to move quick Colonel. We only have eighteen minutes to make our rendezvous with that chopper."

"Maybe our luck is changing," Patton said as he spotted a jeep coming their way.

Before he could finish his thought, three more jeeps came into view. They all pulled up right in front of the building where Patton and his men were hiding, with two Iraqi soldiers in each jeep. Six of the eight Iraqi soldiers ran in the front door, and the other two started circling the building, heading in opposite directions.

Captain Parker, Sergeant Keith Turner, and Jimmy Wilson disappeared into the shadows as Patton waved them back. Coiled and ready to pounce, Patton waited for the soldier to come closer. As the Iraqi came into range, he struck with cat-like quickness. In what seemed like one motion, Patton delivered a ferocious blow to the soldier's midsection, snatched the weapon from his grasp, and caught him under the chin with the butt of the rifle. Patton could hear the air leaving the Iraqi soldier's body, which was doubled over from the force of the first blow. The soldier's chin turned into red pulp as he slid down the side of the building from the force of the second blow.

"We have to get moving," said Patton. "That other guard will be coming around the building at any moment. Bobby, carry the prisoner to the last jeep. Keith, you and I will follow Bobby, but I want you to drive. Jimmy, take care of the other three jeeps. Let's move!"

Bobby picked up the unconscious prisoner, flung him over his shoulder and headed for the jeep. Patton and Keith back peddled out behind him. With their pistols drawn, they never removed their eyes from the building. Jimmy headed to the other jeeps as instructed. Bobby tossed the prisoner into the back of the jeep and hopped in beside him. Keith jumped behind the wheel and started the engine as Patton got in. Jimmy tossed live grenades into the other three jeeps and was running to catch up to the others.

As he jumped in the jeep, the second Iraqi soldier emerged from the shadows of the building and saw them pulling off. He yelled something in Arabic and ran out with his rifle drawn to get a clear shot. Before he could squeeze the trigger, the Iraqi jeeps began to explode, igniting him like a gas-soaked torch. His comrades stormed out of the building but were too late to be of any help. Placing their hands over their noses, they watched in anger as the Iraqi soldier melted into a pile of burning flesh. The Americans vanished into the night.

The jeep came to an abrupt stop in the middle of the desert. All eyes searched the sky as they listened for the sound of a helicopter. After a few long moments, they could hear the whirling blades, faint and far away. Keith flashed the headlights a few times to signal their location. Everyone was looking skyward; no one noticed as the prisoner reached into his boot. He pulled out a knife that had gone undetected during an earlier search and forced it deep into Jimmy's chest. The soft muffled sound of a blade piercing human flesh was one they were all very familiar with.

Patton, Bobby and Keith painfully redirected their attention to the prisoner. His hand was still twisting the blade into Jimmy's body.

Bobby snatched him off of Jimmy and delivered a powerful blow to his head. Jimmy fell from the jeep, never uttering a sound. Patton hurried over to check on his sergeant. He pulled the knife from his chest and applied pressure to the wound.

"We should have nuked this place during Desert Storm." Jimmy mumbled.

"Relax, the chopper's landing, you'll be playing with your kids in no time."

Jimmy smiled at the remark about his kids. He could hardly wait to see his family, but he was so very tired. He just wanted to rest for a few more moments. Everything was moving in slow motion. He could see his colonel saying something to him but he could not hear his words. He saw Bobby deliver several vicious blows to the prisoner, but he did not hear them connect. The helicopter, which had been descending in the distance, had suddenly stopped in mid-air, about ten feet off the ground. He could not hear anything or see any type of movement. To Jimmy, everything looked like a picture … a snapshot that had started to darken. The last image he saw was his wife and kids running out to greet him as he arrived home. His body relaxed and he slowly closed his eyes.

Engulfed with anger, and charging with the intent to kill, Patton jumped up and immediately went after the prisoner. Bobby had already rendered him unconscious, but Patton started to choke him anyway. Bobby and Keith struggled to pull Patton's hands from the man's throat.

"We've got to go," said Bobby, "the cavalry is coming!"

He pointed back behind them. Six pairs of headlights were coming their way. They had about two minutes before the Iraqis would be upon them.

"Let's get out of here," growled Patton.

Before he picked up Jimmy's lifeless body, he yanked two chains from his neck; one contained his dog tags, and the other was the squad's good luck charm, an old Indian-head nickel, with an Indian head on one side and a buffalo on the other. Dooley, Patton's commanding officer, liked the old Buffalo Soldiers and ordered each of his men to wear one of these nickels. Dooley felt that the coin helped unify the platoon and brought them luck. Dooley's men became known as the Buffalo Soldiers and were always sent on the most dangerous assignments. Until now, the old nickels had always brought everyone back alive.

Bobby slung the Iraqi over his shoulder like a bag of potatoes and headed for the helicopter. Keith was the first one in. He jumped in and took Jimmy's body from Patton. Bobby threw the prisoner in the helicopter with no regard to his personal safety and then quickly jumped in himself. He then extended his hand to Patton and helped him in. They were in the helicopter and off the ground in less than thirty seconds. When the Iraqi soldiers arrived, the helicopter was a faint sound in the distant night sky.

"A hell of a retirement party," Patton snapped as Keith tied the hands and feet of the prisoner. "I wonder what other little surprises Dooley has in store for us."

Three days later, Patton, Bobby and Keith arrived at the Pentagon. They had been ordered to report immediately to General Dooley. Patton had already decided that would be his first stop anyway. When they entered Dooley's outer office, Rachel, the general's administrative assistant, knew exactly who they were.

"Have a seat," she said. "General Dooley will be with you in a minute."

Patton continued toward Dooley's office, as if Rachel was invisible. He walked directly past her desk without hesitation. He did not say a word, never glanced in her direction or acknowledged in any way that she was in the room.

"You can't go in there..." but before she could finish her statement, Patton opened the door to Dooley's office and was staring directly at the general. Bobby and Keith were right behind him.

"Something has come up that requires my immediate attention. I'll be in touch," Dooley said before he hung up the telephone.

Patton tossed the dog tags and the Indian-head necklaces of the three men he had lost onto Dooley's desk. "Twenty-eight days! Twenty-eight pleasant, sun filled spring days! That's all the time we had left in the Corps, and you send us into the heart of Iraq on some self-serving suicide mission."

"I think you had better compose yourself, Colonel. It would be a damn shame if you were dishonorably discharged with less than two weeks of service left."

"General, that is the only thing keeping me from planting my boot in your ass. There is only one thing you really wanted to accomplish back there. You were counting on us not making it back. You didn't have to send innocent men to their death because you have a gripe with me. If you were a real man, you wouldn't use the Corps to do your dirty work."

"Patton, so help me God I'll…"

Patton didn't hear him complete his threat; he turned and walked out. Bobby and Keith followed closely behind. Dooley was so angry he couldn't speak. His mouth opened and closed, but nothing came out. His face turned beet red, and he looked as if he was going to burst.

"You're too emotional," Bobby said as they walked down the corridor. "You do too much talking. You should have just gone in, decked him, and went on about your business."

"Well if I don't hurry up and get the hell out of here that is still a possibility."

A couple of months later Patton received a certified letter from Lieutenant Lewis, an information specialist who had served with him in the Corps. The document he pulled from the brown envelope was stamped "Confidential." As he read it, he realized why the lieutenant waited until he was out of the Corp before sending it to him. Patton's hatred for General Stewart Dooley was now stronger than ever, and it would be something that he would carry with him to his grave.

"That low-life son-of-a-bitch! I could kill him with my bare hands."

CHAPTER TWO

As Dale Patton paced the floor, the memories of that last mission consumed his thoughts. It had been twenty years since Sergeant Wilson died in his arms, but he remembered it as if it were yesterday.

Waiting was not one of his strong suits. In a few hours he would be the newly elected President of the United States, unless he lost to Senator Stewart Dooley, the person he despised most in the world.

"Come on Senator, have a seat," said Tommy, as he pulled out a chair. "The pacing is making me dizzy. I have never seen you so nervous."

This was Tommy Granger. Reputed to have one of the sharpest minds in the country, Tommy had always loved politics. The two men had met a few years earlier before Patton had finalized his decision to run for president. They both loved to talk strategy.

"I'm not nervous, I'm angry! Dooley is a piece of shit. If I lose to that son-of-a…"

"I told you, Senator; I don't lose."

"That sounds real good Tommy, but I know of a few senate races that didn't go quite the way you wanted."

"Those idiots lost; I didn't. They did just the opposite of everything I instructed them to do. You, on the other hand, have followed my instructions to the letter. Therefore, victory is assured."

"Can I have that in writing?"

"Relax Senator. Join us for a few hands of poker."

On Tommy's right sat Bobby Parker, and to his left sat Darrin Lewis. Bobby was Patton's best friend. He ran a personal security service that was second to none. Patton hired Bobby and his company as his personal bodyguards after he won the Democratic Primary. He trusted Bobby more than he did the Secret Service. They were on that mission together and, Bobby hated Senator Dooley as much as Patton.

Darrin Lewis was Patton's running mate. He had also served under Dooley with Patton and Bobby. While Patton and Bobby had been warriors, Darrin was more cerebral. He had an I.Q. of 175 and knew a little bit about everything.

Patton and Bobby shared a smile.

"No thanks," said Patton, "I'm a lousy poker player."

"What's with the smiles?" Tommy asked, "Are you really an excellent player trying to bait me?"

"Nah," said Bobby, "he's telling you the truth. He really is a lousy poker player."

"Then what's with these sneaky grins?"

"Should I tell him Dale?"

"Not today. Let's keep him in suspense in case I ever play him."

"I still think you're setting me up for something, but I'll give you a rain-check."

Tommy knew the smile they shared meant something that probably only the two of them and Darrin knew the meaning of, but he would pry no further. He made a mental note to find out what this was all about.

"Well," Patton said, "let's go and watch the results. After all, I have loyal supporters who are waiting to congratulate me on my victory. I just hope they get the opportunity."

Patton knew he shouldn't address or mingle with his supporters until the final results had been announced, but he was tired of waiting. Bobby grabbed his special infra-red sunglasses from the table and hurried out in front of Patton. His dark glasses and headset was his trademark. There were very few times when he was without either, not to mention his pearl handled nine-millimeter pistol. That's probably because he always seemed to be working. At six feet, 190 pounds, Bobby looked as if he had been chiseled from a piece of brown clay. He was muscular but not stiff. He had a thin mustache and a military haircut, and his clothes were always loose fitting and comfortable, for freedom of movement.

Born and raised in Atlanta, Bobby joined the Marine Corps at the age of eighteen. That was where he first met Dale Patton. Their similar interest in high school football and martial arts, not to mention their mutual hatred of General Dooley, started a lifelong friendship.

Bobby's memory of Atlanta is 180 degrees from how the area is depicted today, especially his neighborhood. He was the typical, poor, black man from the hood who made something of himself. Bobby took his share of lumps growing up, but he dished out more than he received. He used to fight so much that he began to like it. Why not? He became good at it. He earned respect through fear and was quickly heading down the wrong path. Though his mother couldn't afford it, she forced him to take martial arts lessons to give him some discipline and keep him off the streets.

The martial arts calmed him down but didn't change him. He developed into a calm, calculating hoodlum, instead of a mature, humble man. He realized he wasn't as tough as he thought he was when he made the mistake of jumping his instructor out of anger. That was the worst, and last, beating Bobby ever received.

After his wounds healed, his anger consumed him with thoughts of revenge. Bobby was so angry that he had thought about getting a pistol and killing his instructor. However, he didn't want to go down that path. He realized he needed help, so he joined the Marines. After a few successful years, he was transferred into Patton's unit, an elite fighting group that handled only special assignments. Colonel Dale Patton became the first man Bobby trusted, respected, and looked up to. They had been virtually inseparable ever since.

Patton was similar in stature to Bobby, but not as muscular. Always in good physical condition, he stood six feet, 175 pounds, had dark brown hair, and was clean-shaven. He was born and raised in Charlotte, North Carolina. He was nine years older than Bobby and had finished college before entering the service. His handsome features and designer suits camouflaged his competitive demeanor. People often underestimated him because of his appearance. First, last and foremost, Dale Patton was a soldier, a strategic genius. Like any strategist, he loved to be underestimated. His clean cut, Ivy-League, rich boy look made him appear soft. By the time an adversary found out any different, he had been outwitted and defeated. He was a natural leader, demanding to work for but well liked.

Patton's enlistment into the Corps was for personal reasons, but he was driven by a different purpose. His father was a career soldier and wanted his oldest child to follow in his footsteps. Patton loved and respected his father, but he wanted to blaze his own path. He had the same servant spirit but wanted to be a lawyer. He disliked bullies, and at that time, the local police department had the reputation of being just that. Too many cases of Police brutality had gone unpunished in his community, and Patton wanted to put a stop to it. He saw them as bullies hiding behind their badges.

Patton went to college and received his undergraduate degree. However, the year before he graduated, his father died in a military training exercise. Patton felt bad that he had not followed his father into the service. He felt his father had been disappointed in him.

Just a couple of months before he was to start law school, Patton's life changed forever. His younger brother was killed in a robbery at the bank where he worked. John was working as a teller to pay his own way through school. He had complied with the robbers' demands and was not resisting in any way, but when one of the thugs recognized him as the son of Victor Patton, the local war hero, they began to harass him. John kept his cool until they started to demean his father's accomplishments. He politely suggested that the thugs kiss his ass, and one of them shot him at point-blank range. John was dead before he hit the floor.

Patton did not handle his brother's death very well. He had lost his father and brother a little more than a year apart. He began to display anger he didn't know he possessed. He had to be physically restrained when he went to the trial and saw the punk that shot his brother. He lingered around the house with his mother for months. Law school

WILLIAM I. BRAZLEY JR.

didn't appeal to him anymore. He still hated bullies, but there had to be a better, faster way to appease his anger.

The Marine Corp was that way. He could honor his father and avenge his brother at the same time. The Special Forces was his goal going in. They went after the bad guys, the bullies.

Darrin Lewis followed Patton onto the floor. Lewis looked more like an aristocrat and could have run for president on his own merits.

He had thought about running but concluded that the country was not quite ready for another African American President. President Obama had done well and he would be a tough act to follow. When Patton asked him to be his vice-president, he quickly accepted. This way, the country would continue to see a black man in the White House, and he could use the experience and the exposure to his benefit. He and Patton together would be a hard team to beat.

At six feet two inches tall and a hundred and ninety-five pounds, Darrin had chocolate brown skin and was very distinguished looking. His black, gray streaked hair and wire rim glasses gave him a very distinguished and trustworthy appearance. The physical challenges of the Marine Corps posed a few problems for him, but his knowledge of the law, of military rules and regulations and of the military code of ethics kept him, Bobby and Patton out of serious trouble on more than a few occasions. A recognized authority on human behavior and political science, Lewis served primarily as a personal advisor. A job not usually given to the vice-president, but it was one Patton would add to his other responsibilities.

Last in line came Tommy Granger. Tommy was Patton's campaign manager; he had known Patton for about three years and was hired for one reason and one reason only; to win the election. Patton liked Tommy but did not completely trust him. Tommy had many contacts; some of whom were very seedy characters. He could to get any piece of information he wanted. He was not nearly as physically fit as the other three. He was five feet eight inches tall, 180 pounds, clean-shaven, with black hair and a potbelly.

When the four of them entered the room more than two hundred supporters greeted them with chants and cheers. The likeness of Patton on signs, posters, and campaign buttons could be seen everywhere. Members of the press were present. There were two large, flat screen televisions on the wall in the rear of the room. They were showing minute by minute election results.

On their way to the podium, Katie Patton, the candidate's wife, and her mother, Katherine Morrison, caught up to them. Katie was a very attractive woman. She was strong, assertive, independent, and somewhat of a celebrity in her own right. Born to a wealthy family, she served on several national committees and had always been pro-family. Though she had no kids of her own, her unwavering views of a strong, cohesive family unit were well documented. Katie met Patton in college and was there for him during that very tough year. She stayed in touch with him when he joined the Marines. They married a couple of years later when he came home on leave.

Katherine was the stereotypical mother-in-law. She was forever interfering in everyone's business, and she and Patton were always at odds about something. She was not bad looking for a woman in her mid-sixties. Her sandy-brown hair and green eyes gave her an angelic appearance, which was very misleading. Katherine would literally take over if she was not dealt with firmly.

"Is it all over, am I the next President," Patton asked his wife as she approached him?

"Not far from it," Katie replied, "you are ahead by twenty electoral votes. We are waiting for the results from California. If the pre-election estimates are correct about you and Dooley splitting California, you will be the next President."

"Dale, when you win, what will my responsibilities be as the first mother-in-law," asked Katherine?

"How long before we get the results from California," Patton asked, ignoring his mother-in-law?

"Not too long, a couple more hours."

"Well, I have been waiting for eighteen months. I guess I can wait a couple more hours."

Tommy chimed in. "I told you that a victory is guaranteed. Just relax and concentrate on your victory speech."

"When you make that speech don't forget to mention how big of an influence your mother-in-law is, Katherine said. "By the way, why did I have trouble getting in here tonight? If it wasn't for Bobby, I would probably be sitting in some dark cell with my hands cuffed behind my back."

"Just a mix-up Mom, I thought you were going on a trip."

"Don't worry about my trip," she snapped. "I'm going right after we move into the White House. Mix-up my ass! I need a drink. And don't call me Mom." Trying to hide a smile, Katherine winked at Patton as she walked off.

"Come on," said Tommy as he motioned Patton and Darrin toward the platform. "You two should be up there, where everyone can see you."

CHAPTER THREE

Stewart Dooley slowly walked down the steps of the platform. The room was quiet, deathly quiet. The large screen television in the rear of the room had just given the results from California. What had been a party just moments earlier was now a wake. The cheers were now whispers. The bragging and boasting had turned into apologies. As far as the election was concerned, Stewart Dooley was dead and buried. His supporters began to clear the room. Michelle Mason, the Channel 8 News anchor from D.C., caught up to the defeated GOP candidate. Microphone in hand, Michelle cued her cameraman.

"What went wrong General," she asked? "According to the experts, you should have won by a comfortable margin."

Senator Dooley was a large man. He stood six feet three inches tall and weighed 240 pounds. His bald head and thick mustache enhanced his intimidating demeanor.

"It's Senator Dooley," he snapped. "As far as those so-called experts are concerned, I think they should be reevaluated."

"Senator, rumor has it that there is bad blood between you and the president-elect. As a Senator from Virginia, how will that affect your working relationship, especially since he used to follow your orders and now you must take orders from him?"

Dooley fixed his full attention on the news anchor. His eyes squinted and his jaws tightened as he started to speak through clenched teeth. His lips parted for an instant, but he closed his mouth in a hurry, struggling to regain his composure.

"First of all, I don't take orders from anyone. Dale Patton needs my experience and leadership. As far as bad blood goes, you will have to talk to him about that. He had problems taking orders from me, yet he was considered a hero when he left the service. If I emerge from his leadership in half as good a shape as he emerged from mine, I'll be satisfied. Excuse me, Ms. Mason, I must be going."

Dooley turned and walked away before she could respond. Plowing his way through some of his die-hard supporters, he managed a swift exit. Upon reaching the elevators he repeatedly pressed the down button. When the doors finally opened, he entered and continued his assault on the button for the first floor.

"Me take orders from Dale Patton," he mumbled. "It's not over yet, Dale. Enjoy it while you can."

The television camera crews came alive as soon as it was announced that Patton had won California. Photographers pushed and shoved to get better angles for their shots. The media had surrounded the platform, each reporter trying to get the first interview with the next President of the United States.

Tommy grinned from ear to ear as Patton and Darrin waved to their supporters. He walked over to them and shook both of their hands. "I told you victory was assured. Congratulations Mr. President!"

"Thanks Tommy, this wouldn't have been possible without you."

Tommy believed that Patton was truly grateful. He knew Patton would be a great President, and to have him in his debt was his greatest achievement. He could ask for almost anything, within reason of course. He would think it over carefully. By the time the inauguration took place, he would know what he wanted.

Patton and Darrin continued to wave to the crowd. They joined hands and held their arms over their heads, giving photographers the front-page picture of every newspaper across the country. Both of their wives, and Katherine, were with them on stage. Katherine walked over to her son-in-law, squeezed herself between Katie and Patton, and put her arm around his waist. She smiled and waved as if she were the first lady.

Tommy went to the front of the platform and called for order. After a while, he finally got the noise level down low enough so that he could be heard.

"Thank you, ladies and gentlemen for that generous applause; thanks to all of you, the best man did win. I know that Dale Patton will be a great President, as time will surely confirm. Now, without further delay, I give you the next President of the United States, President-Elect Dale Patton."

The room erupted into cheers and applause all over again. He waved to all of his supporters and mouthed the words thank you. Bobby spoke into his headset and bodyguards appeared out of nowhere. They surrounded the platform and kept everyone a safe distance from the newly elected president.

"The first thing I want to say is thank-you," said Patton. "I am not very fond of long speeches. I was once told that a man who talks a lot accomplishes very little. You already know, from my campaign what my agenda is. I want affordable healthcare. I want a lower crime rate and a higher employment rate. Economic recovery is at the top of my agenda because I care about people. As wealthy as this country is, hunger and homelessness should not be something our citizens have to experience. We have to take care of our own. Damn the whales; save the people!"

The room ignited into instant applause and the flashing of the cameras was almost blinding.

"I want to thank you again for your support. It is greatly appreciated. I have a lot of work to do, and I must be going."

"Mr. President, what do you think will be your first official duty?" shouted a reporter from the floor.

"I will probably ask Senator Dooley to resign. Thank you ladies and gentlemen, that's all the time I have."

The room fell silent for a moment, as Patton headed toward the exit. Bobby and his men led the presidential party out of the room while reporters were scribbling notes regarding Patton's last statement. The crowd burst into applause once more as the presidential party was led out the door.

CHAPTER FOUR

It was unseasonably warm for Washington D.C. this time of year. Usually January temperatures were well below freezing. Today, however, for Patton's inauguration, it was a sunny, comfortable 48 degrees. The Whitehouse lawn had been prepared for the large crowd that was now waiting to see the next President sworn into office. This group consisted entirely of politicians, high-ranking officials, and their families. There was an even larger gathering peering through the fencing around the grounds.

"Raise your right hand and repeat after me," instructed the Chief Justice.

Patton took the oath of office and was sworn in as President of the United States. That was the only part of his inauguration that he really looked forward to. The rest of the festivities took place that night at a private reception, but he hated to be around phony people who smiled and shook his hand, all the while hoping he would fall flat on his face, or people who were only there for their own self-serving reasons. He was not very fond of political protocol. This was a part of his job he knew he would not perform well.

"Hello Mr. President, do you have a few moments for the first lady," asked Katie as she and Katherine approached?

"Always," he replied, and then he whispered, "Where did you get that scare crow. I can have Bobby shoot her if she is bothering you."

"Behave Dale; don't get Mother started."

"I'll tell you what. It will take more than Bobby to pull me off of you."

"Why Katherine, what big ears you have."

Bobby smiled. He knew Patton was totally enjoying himself at this moment, probably the first time all night.

"Let me tell you something, boy…."

"You two stop this instant," demanded Katie. "Mother, shouldn't you be getting ready to catch your plane?"

"You're right dear. I won't let that jackass ruin my vacation. I will see you in about three weeks. Make sure my room in the big house is ready by then."

Katherine winked at Patton as she hugged her daughter good-bye, and then turned and began to leave. As she walked away Bobby spoke into his headset. Two Secret Service agents emerged from the crowd and escorted Katherine out.

"What is she taking a vacation from?" asked Patton, "she doesn't do anything."

"Dale, why can't you get along with Mother?"

"I think we get along very well. We have a perfect understanding. Where is she going anyway?"

"She's going to visit the Holy Land, Israel, Jerusalem, and Egypt. This is something she has always wanted to do."

"She's going by herself?"

"No, a friend of hers, Ruth Wilcox, is meeting her in New York. They have known each other forever."

"Well, Bobby, at least she is out of your hair for a while."

"Your mother-in-law is never a problem, Mr. President," Bobby said with a wide smile across his face.

"Good answer," said Patton, who could not keep from laughing.

"I am glad everyone is having such a good time," Katie said. "I think I will mingle a little so everyone can speak freely. Mr. President I will speak with you later."

Bobby knew Katie wasn't upset. She played along to allow Patton to enjoy himself. Katie and Bobby got along very well. They genuinely liked and trusted each other. That was one thing Patton was truly grateful for.

Getting Bobby as his personal bodyguard was another thing that brought him great satisfaction. Only Secret Service agents could guard the President. The only way Patton could have Bobby and his men assigned to him was to have them join the Secret Service. The background checks were not a problem. The problem was persuading Homeland Security to work with him. Patton considered this his first victory as President.

His first official act, and the biggest pleasure of his life, would come in the morning. Asking Dooley to step down was something he had looked forward to for a long time.

"Hello Mr. President," greeted Tommy. "I hope you are enjoying yourself?"

"Not really, this is one part of the job I don't particularly care for."

Tommy had known Patton for some time now, and his honest, straightforward approach often caught him off guard. For some reason Patton kept him at a distance. He seemed to always have his guard up whenever they were around each other. Tommy knew that he would never be as close to Patton as Bobby was, but he wanted a little more than just a working relationship. It would take time before the President completely trusted him. That made this meeting even more uncomfortable.

"I was wondering if you have had the time to consider my request. I know this is not the best time to bring this up, but press secretary is a position you really should fill as soon as possible."

"Yes Tommy, I have made a decision. I will grant your request. However, there is something I would like to emphasize."

"What is it?"

"Any time you speak on my behalf, your words must have the same tone and intensity as my words. Your statements must never soften or harden the message I dictate to you. Make sure you know exactly how I feel about every situation before you attribute any statements to me publicly. Understood?"

"Understood, and thank you. I won't let you down."

Tommy walked away, very happy and very relieved. He knew Patton meant exactly what he said. He also knew he would not have been appointed the president's press secretary out of mere gratitude. He felt better, but the conversation was a little too formal. He felt as if he had to prove himself again. He would concern himself with that another time. Tonight, he would enjoy himself.

The next morning, Patton was up early, ready to start his first day on the job. He sat behind his desk in the Oval Office, deep in thought. Stewart Dooley was on his way down. There were so many things he wanted to say to him, but he wasn't sure where to start. The trouble between the two of them started back in 1993, after the parking garage in the World Trade Center was bombed.

One of the terrorists was identified, and the CIA soon discovered that he was hiding in Iraq. In fact, the United States believed Iraq was retaliating for the devastation its country endured during the Gulf War. Patton believed this was the opportunity Dooley had been looking for to further his own career. Dooley believed that he and his men were expendable to highlight his personal resume. Three men died needlessly. Twenty years later, those memories still angered the newly elected president.

"Mr. President, Senator Dooley is here to see you," said a voice over the intercom.

He stared at the intercom box for a few moments without saying a word. The voice had brought him back from the past.

"Mr. President?" repeated the voice.

"Thanks Sarah, send the Senator in, and ask Bobby to step in also please."

"As you wish, sir."

"Sarah, make sure we are not interrupted."

"Yes sir."

Senator Stewart Dooley walked into the Oval Office, followed by Bobby, who closed the door behind him. He stood with his back to the door and his hands cupped behind his back. He knew Patton did not need him in the room. He had allowed him to be present as more of a favor than anything else. Bobby would not have missed this for anything in the world.

"Good morning General, how have you been," asked Patton?

"It's Senator now, Dale, or should I call you Mr. President?"

"Yes it is Senator isn't it, but I think you prefer General. And yes, call me Mr. President."

"Don't hold your breath."

"Now Senator, you should have more respect for the country's executive officer."

"Is that what this is all about? You called me down here to rub your victory in my face? I didn't think you were that shallow. I hope you are about finished, because I have matters to attend to."

"Well, Senator, I hope you can finish those matters by the end of the week, because I want you to turn in your resignation. I don't want to see you in Washington ever again."

"Is that some sort of sick joke? You think you can make me tuck my tail and run just because you are the President? It will take a better man than you to threaten me."

"I don't threaten people, Dooley. Do you remember Operation Manhattan?"

"I can't say that I do."

"A bit of amnesia huh? Well, let me refresh your memory. I'm talking about a covert operation back in 1993 in which three men died. Two had a wife and kids."

"Well, war is hell."

"That's the problem. We were not in a war at the time. Three men died for nothing, because the mission was unnecessary. Are you starting to remember now?"

"Stop wasting my time Dale, and get to the point."

"The point is Iraq had already agreed to extradite that man, and you were aware of that. There was no need for a covert mission. The way I see it, General, you murdered three men."

"Iraq agreed to a lot of things they reneged on. Besides, that was classified information. You have no proof."

"That's where you are wrong. You forgot about Lieutenant Darrin Lewis. Do you remember him? He is the Vice-President now. Darrin was privilege to a lot of classified information. What you didn't realize was how close we are-Darrin, Bobby, and I."

"You still don't have anything on me. It's just his word against mine."

"I have more than just his word. I have a copy of the original letter, which verifies everything I just said. That letter will be in every newspaper in the country if you are not off the hill by the end of the week."

"You're bluffing."

Patton and Bobby made quick eye contact. They both smiled for a split-second, and then Patton stood up and looked Dooley square in the eyes.

"If I do not hear word of your resignation from the Senate by the end of the week, I will have you arrested and indicted for murder."

"You two are really enjoying this aren't you?"

"I am. How about you Bobby?"

"I will enjoy it more at the end of the week."

"You arrogant son-of-a-bitch! How dare you try to humiliate me like this? It will take a better man than you to run me out of town. If you come after me, Dale, you better know what you're doing. A soft fellow like you can't take a lot of heat."

"You don't have to run out of town, General; you can walk. Have a nice day. By the way, any time you think I am too soft, try your luck."

The two men stared at each other. Dooley's face turned red with anger, and his jaws tightened. Bobby brought his arms to his side and took a step forward when Dooley clenched his fists. Patton continued to make eye contact but did not move a muscle. Dooley slowly opened his hands, turned, and walked toward the door. Bobby did not move an inch as he blocked Dooley's path.

"Mr. President," he asked, "are you finished with the General?"

"Yes, unless you have something you would like to say to him."

Except for smiling a wide grin, Bobby did not budge. After a few moments, he stepped to one side and allowed Dooley to leave. Halfway down the hall, the media met Dooley. He plowed right through them, not giving anyone an opportunity to ask a question. Bobby closed the door.

"You know," said Patton, "that would have been really cruel had that been anyone but Dooley. I have angered many a person, but that is the first time I enjoyed it."

"That's because we both know he deserved every minute of it. It was long overdue. I only wish he had given me a reason to knock him on his ass. That would have felt really good."

"As angry as he is right now, you might get the opportunity in the near future. You know the man lives for revenge."

"I hope you are right. I would love to go heads up with him. However, maybe that's not a good idea. If that ever happened, I know I wouldn't stop until I ripped his heart from his chest."

"Let's hope we have seen the last of General Stewart Dooley. Now, let me see, what's next on my agenda? Whatever it is, it won't be nearly as much fun."

Dooley slammed the outer office door as he walked toward his office. He removed his jacket, flung it across the room, and sat down behind his desk.

"Dale Patton must pay," he said. I don't know how, but the man must suffer, and it has to happen soon. No one orders me to pack my bags and leave, not even the President of the United States."

Dooley was past angry. He was irate. Both of his hands were balled into fists, resting on the arms of his brown leather chair. His squinty eyes and clenched teeth caused veins to bulge from his forehead. His face was so red it that looked as if it was going to explode. Cold sweat ran down his face. His breathing became shallow and labored. He looked as if he was going to go into cardiac arrest. The telephone rang, causing him to refocus. That call may have saved his life.

"What?" he growled into the phone.

"Senator," answered Rachel, "Michelle Mason from Channel 8 News wants to speak to you. She claims it is extremely important."

Rachel had been with him since his days at the Pentagon, when he first became a general. He brought her with him to D.C. when he became a Senator. They were a good match. She was probably the only person able to put up with him.

"Hold all of my calls. I don't want to speak to anyone until further notice. There are no exceptions. Do you understand?"

"Yes Senator."

"A reporter is the last person I want to speak to," he mumbled as he slammed down the telephone. "That son-of-a-bitch probably called her as soon as I left the Oval Office."

Dooley picked up the telephone and made a call. He tapped his fingers impatiently as he waited for the party on the other end to answer.

"Listen and listen well," he commanded. "I want to know every move the President makes. Keep me informed of everything."

"Anything in particular?" asked the voice on the other end.

"Yes," replied Dooley, "anything I can use against him."

Dooley pressed the button to end the call, and then quickly dialed another number.

"I want to speak to Bill Pitts. Tell him Stewart Dooley is on the phone."

After a momentary pause, Bill Pitts answered. "Make it quick Stewart; I'm heading out the door."

"Bill, I have to see you before you leave. It's extremely important."

"I can stop by on my way out, in about thirty minutes."

"Great, I'll see you then."

Bill Pitts was head of the CIA.

CHAPTER FIVE

Ockbar Shalam smoked a cigarette as he looked out over the dark runway. The time was near, and everything had to be perfect. So far things had gone as planned, but it had all been easy, up until now. The waiting was the hard part. The real test would soon be at hand, and mistakes would not be tolerated. They would be punishable by death. Everyone knew exactly what was expected of them. Failure was not an option.

A moan in the back of the building caught Ockbar's attention. He walked toward the back of the hangar. Lying on the floor were five men, dressed only in their underwear and t-shirts and covered with blood. Their throats had been slit, and they had been left for dead. Apparently one of them was still alive. The man was barely conscious, writhing in pain.

Ockbar took a draw from his cigarette, pulled a six-inch blade from his boot, and stabbed the helpless victim twice in the chest. Blood gurgled from the cut in the victim's throat and spilled from his mouth with each impact of the knife. He slumped over, motionless. Ockbar wiped the blade clean on the dead man's shirt and put the knife back in his boot. After flicking ashes in the face of the corpse, he returned to his men.

He uttered something in their native tongue and pointed back over his shoulder. They all shared a good laugh. One man spat in the direction of the slain ground crew. This continued for a few minutes until Ockbar checked his watch. It was time. He issued a command, and the men began to inspect their equipment. They all pulled out semi-automatic weapons, ammunition, and explosives. All of their pistols had silencers attached to them. They concealed their pistols in their uniforms, which had been taken from the ground crew. Ockbar removed a cell phone from one of the bags and put it in his pocket. They all watched as a plane approached the runway.

"Will everyone please fasten your seatbelt," the pilot instructed over the intercom. "We will be landing at Cairo International Airport in five minutes. For those of you headed to Israel, you have about forty-five minutes to catch your connecting flight. Thank you for flying American World Airlines."

Ruth Wilcox had followed the pilot's instructions to the letter. She could not ever remember feeling so fatigued from just sitting. Her arthritis had started bothering her an hour earlier, and she had been miserable ever since. She started rubbing her arms and legs to increase the circulation and eliminate the stiffness she felt in her joints. She looked over at Katherine Morrison, who was sleeping as if she hadn't a care in the world. The three cocktails she had consumed within the last hour probably had a lot to do with her peaceful slumber.

"Wake up," Ruth said as she nudged Katherine. "Fasten your seatbelt. We are about to land." Katherine did not move.

"Wake up," Ruth repeated, trying to shake her friend awake. "We are about to land."

Katherine mumbled something unrecognizable and turned toward the window. Ruth reached over and fastened Katherine's seatbelt. They only had about fifteen minutes before they would have to leave the plane. Ruth sat back and tried to think of a way to wake her friend. Worse-case scenario, she would ask the two Secret Service Agents, Joe and Charlie, to carry Katherine from the plane. However, that would be too embarrassing, so she decided against it.

When the plane touched down, the ground crew was in place. Ockbar was out front with lights, guiding the plane in. Two other men pulled up in a fuel truck, ready to refuel it. Two additional men had rolled out the steps and were ready to position them at the door of the aircraft. When the plane came to a complete stop, the two men in the fuel truck went to work. The other two rolled the steps into place, and then one of the men quickly ran up the steps. As he reached the door, it swung open. The gunman stuck his pistol into the ribs of the flight attendant and forced her back inside. A few seconds later, a second gunman entered the plane, brandishing his weapon also. Each man pointed his weapon down opposite sides of the aircraft. They were daring anyone to move.

Ockbar entered with his pistol drawn and eyes on the cockpit. He motioned to one of the gunmen, who turned and kicked open the door of the cockpit. The pilot and co-pilot found themselves staring down the barrel of a nine-millimeter pistol. In broken English, the flight crew was instructed to remove their headsets and to sit on their hands. The co-pilot began to speak, but without warning, the gunman struck him across the face with his pistol. The co-pilot fell to the floor as blood trickled from a large gash on his left cheek. The other pilot did as he was instructed.

The passengers began to panic when they saw pistols waving back and forth. Their captors called for silence and pointed their weapons at anyone who was not quiet. Joe and Charlie made eye contact. There were too many unknowns, and this was not the time to act. At that moment, a fourth gunman boarded the plane. He said something to Ockbar, who answered, and then the gunman left the plane.

Ruth was scared speechless. She was as white as a ghost. Katherine would pick this particular moment to awaken. She was yawning and stretching as if she was fully rested. Ruth prayed her friend would not cause any trouble, but it never failed, Katherine had to be the center of attention, even when she was waking up. Everyone watched her as she stirred from her sleep.

The Secret Service Agents were the most concerned. She was a handful, even when she tried to be cooperative. They just hoped she recognized the situation for what it was and not cause trouble, at least not until they could get clear shots at the gunmen. Their worst fears began to materialize as Katherine stood up and began to look around.

"Where are we?" she asked. "Where the hell did you gorillas come from?" She made eye contact with Ockbar and added, "You look like you may just be dumb enough to be the leader."

"You are very perceptive, madam. Now sit back down and shut up before I blow your head off."

"You don't scare me, you…"

"Calm down, dear," interrupted Charlie, "I believe these gentlemen mean business."

"Yes," Ruth said nervously. "We should do as they say."

Charlie gave Katherine a stern look, as she sat down, hoping she got the message. This was not the time to be obstinate. She was putting people's lives in danger. He hoped she realized the seriousness of the situation.

"Don't call me dear. You don't know me that well. Why aren't you and Joe doing something? What in the hell are you waiting for?"

Ockbar walked up the aisle to Katherine and pointed his pistol directly at her head.

"No, don't!" yelled Charlie, jumping up from his seat.

Ockbar pointed his pistol at Charlie's chest and squeezed off a round. The passengers screamed uncontrollably. Blood went everywhere. Katherine, Ruth and Joe were splattered as Charlie fell back into his seat. His body convulsed into spasms as his heart had made several powerful beats, trying to revive his body. After what seemed like an eternity, his body relaxed. The pistol made very little noise because of the silencer, but the screaming and crying of the passengers were more frightening than Charlie's blood covered torso.

When Ockbar fired his pistol, Joe stuck his hand under his jacket, more of a reflex than anything else. He then found himself staring down the barrel of Ockbar's smoking pistol. Joe very slowly put both hands in his lap. The gunman who had been standing by the door came down the aisle and jammed his pistol in the back of Joe's head. Ockbar reached over and opened Joe's jacket. He removed his pistol and wallet and examined them.

"Who are these ladies, Joe Campbell, and why do you guard them?"

"They are wealthy American tourists who are afraid to travel in this part of the world alone. You didn't have to shoot this man."

"If you do not tell me the truth, you will be next."

"That is the truth."

"Then why do you carry the standard issue of the Secret Service?"

"How did you know that?"

"Never mind, just answer the question."

"I am retired from the Secret Service, now I work as a personal bodyguard. I was allowed to keep my service pistol as a gift."

Katherine was mortified. She could not stop looking at poor Charlie, slumped down in his seat with blood oozing from a large hole in his chest. She felt sick at the pit of her stomach. Tears streamed down her face. It was all her fault. He would still be alive if she had kept her big mouth shut. She could feel herself start to tremble, but she could not lose her composure. She could not let them know how frightened she really was. She calmed herself and began to wipe the spattered blood from her face.

"You are also a liar," replied Ockbar.

The last gunman boarded the plane, and now all five were on board. One of them said something to Ockbar, who nodded and issued a command. They only spoke in their native tongue when they spoke to each other. One gunman pulled Joe from his seat while the other kept his pistol focused on him. Another one of them removed Charlie's body. Joe watched as Charlie's pistol was taken from its holster and his body was thrown from the plane.

When Joe turned back around to face Ockbar, he felt himself falling backward. Ockbar had fired another round. Joe's left shoulder began to puddle with blood, and all eyes were upon him as he hit the floor with a thud.

"Tell your government that Ockbar wants his brother released. I will contact your government within twenty-four hours. Your delivering this message is the only reason you are still alive. I will have fun finding out who these ladies are on my own."

Ockbar walked over to Joe and ground the heel of his right boot into his shoulder wound. With his pistol pointed at his head, Ockbar continued to grind his heel into the bloody wound until he lost consciousness. Katherine cried heavily as Joe was removed from the plane in the same manner as they had Charlie.

The plane had been refueled and was ready for take-off. Ockbar gave the pilot a new set of coordinates, and then he grabbed the radio and talked to the flight tower.

"Listen and listen well. I will not repeat myself. There are already two bodies on the runway. If this plane is not cleared for immediate takeoff, there will be many more."

Within three minutes, the plane had disappeared into the night.

"Make sure there are no more surprises," ordered Ockbar.

At this command, two of the terrorists began to check each passenger. They inspected every carry-on bag, including the women's purses. Every passenger on board was thoroughly patted down, regardless of their age or gender. Every cell phone, laptop, portable media player, and every other electronic gadget was taken.

CHAPTER SIX

"Politics is something I hope I never get used to," said Patton as he stood up and stretched. "This has truly been an interesting day."

"You have a lot of work ahead of you Dale," Darrin said. "I hope you realize what you're up against?"

"Don't worry. I know exactly what's going on. I don't like the us-against-them mentality this job is forcing me into."

"Just remember why you got into politics in the first place. You always hated politics but realized this was the only way you could right some wrongs. This is where it all starts. We have to stack the deck in our favor to get anything accomplished."

"Don't get me wrong Darrin, I'm not complaining. As a matter of fact, I am looking forward to forming my cabinet and making a few other essential appointments. I enjoy the competition."

"You know you have a lot of opposition. The republicans control the Senate. They oversee the Foreign Relations Committee and the Armed Services Committee. Don't forget about Banking, Housing, and Urban Affairs, not to mention the Speaker of the House."

"I know, I know. Like I said, I enjoy the competition. Besides, Congress doesn't exactly know what to expect from me just yet. I'm sure they think I'll...."

"Mr. President, Tommy Granger is here to see you," interrupted Sarah.

"Darrin and I are about to wrap it up for the day. Tell him I need a few minutes, Sarah."

"Mr. Granger says this is top priority, sir. He says it cannot wait."

"Very well, send him in. Top priority, huh? I wonder what has gotten him so worked up."

"We'll know in a minute."

Tommy came through the door with a very intense look on his face. He walked in a slow, steady pace, as if he was undecided on whether he wanted to be there or not.

"What is so important that the President and Vice-President must be disturbed on our first official day in office," asked Patton.

"Excuse the interruption, Mr. President, but an American plane has been hijacked in Egypt."

Darrin quickly examined the President's demeanor and body language. He knew this was right at the top of the list of the things Patton felt strongly about. Patton always said the United States implemented too much protocol and diplomacy and treated terrorist aggression with kid gloves. He often talked about how far advanced the military was over the rest of the world, and how much some of these terrorist-based, dictator-run countries got away with in the name of peace.

"Give me the details," demanded Patton.

"It happened a few hours ago in Cairo. American World Airlines Flight 454 was taken at the Cairo International Airport. One man has been killed and another has been seriously wounded. The plane has about 212 people on board. We are not sure how many terrorists are on board."

"How much do the media know? Have there been any demands?"

"There have been no demands as of yet. The media knows only that a plane has been hijacked and that two Americans are the dead and wounded. We may have a ten-minute head start before the story hits the international airwaves. Sir, AWA Flight 454 is the plane your mother-in-law is on. One of her bodyguards is dead, and Joe Campbell is wounded. He is still unconscious."

"Katherine is on that plane?"

"Yes sir."

Patton flipped a switch on his desk panel and buzzed his assistant.

"Yes, Mr. President?"

"Sarah, get General Phillips on the line immediately."

"Yes, Mr. President."

"Tommy, why is this information coming from you instead of Bill Pitts or Ray Silva? Shouldn't the head of the CIA or the director of the FBI be informing me of this situation?"

"I doubt if they are aware of it, sir."

"They don't know about it?"

"I doubt it, sir."

Patton and Darrin stared at Tommy. They were both impressed. Tommy was tingling with excitement but showed no outward signs.

"Connections," said Tommy.

"Good work," said Patton.

"Thank you Mr. President."

"Mr. President, General Phillips is on line one," said Sarah.

"Sarah is Bill Pitts still in Washington, or has he gone back to Langley?"

"He should still be here, Mr. President. He is scheduled to leave in about an hour."

"Good, call him and tell him I need to see him ASAP. Also, find my wife and ask her to come down here. Tell her it's an emergency."

"Yes, Mr. President."

"Tommy, handle the media. I do not want them to know any more than they already know, at least not until we can get more information on this situation. I plan to leave for Camp David in about ninety minutes and will keep in touch with you from there. Also, inform the media that Richard Payne is out and that General Phillips is the new Commander of the Joint Chiefs of Staff, pending Senate approval of course. Wait until I have left for Camp David before you hold your press conference."

"As you wish," said Tommy.

Patton picked up the phone as Tommy turned and left the room. "Gary, I need your help."

"What can I do for you, Mr. President?"

"Richard Payne is out. I would like for you to be commander of the joint chiefs."

"This is unprecedented and unexpected. I don't know what to say."

"Say yes."

"Yes, of course, I would be honored, sir."

"Good. A situation has arisen. I need you in my office right away."

"I'm on my way sir."

"Darrin, I want to have a word with Mr. Bill Pitts in private. Instruct Sarah to make sure Air Force One is ready to leave for Camp David within the hour. Find Bobby and brief him and General Phillips on the hijacking. Also, ask Sarah to address a memo to Richard Payne, informing him of his replacement. I want to sign it in fifteen minutes and have it delivered to him before I leave for Camp David. Tell him that an emergency has come up, and I will meet with him in person, if he wishes, after the crisis has been resolved."

"Consider it done, Mr. President. I don't think this will come as a big surprise to Richard Payne. You realize General Phillips is very strong in the Republican Party?"

"I won't hold that against him. We shouldn't have any problem getting him approved by the senate, unless we fail to bring the hostages back alive. Richard Payne has to go. He's one of Dooley's boys."

As Darrin left the room, Bill Pitts was coming in. Darrin greeted him, and then just shook his head as he went on his way. He knew Patton was going to rip him apart, especially since he put up such strong opposition against Bobby and his men joining the Secret Service. Bill Pitts had no clue about the hijacking.

"Bill, how is everything going," asked Patton?

"Just fine, Mr. President."

"Tell me something, Bill. How does the information get to me when there is a crisis involving the US or our citizens abroad?"

"You are usually informed of the situation by the secretary of defense, or one of the chiefs of staff. Sometimes the FBI director, Ray Silva, or I will pass the information along. Why do you ask?"

"I was wondering why none of you informed me of the hijacking of an American tourist plane."

Pitts' blank expression gave him away. He had no idea what the President was talking about. His face started to turn red as he struggled for something intelligent to say. Being uninformed was not good; it was his job to stay informed.

"I didn't know a plane had been hijacked, Mr. President."

The instant he finished his statement, he knew he had said the wrong thing. All he could do was brace himself for Patton's reply.

"That's exactly the problem," snapped Patton. "You should be informing me of these matters. I shouldn't have to inform you. What if there was a plot against my life? When would you know about it, at my funeral?"

"Sir, I assure you…"

"I don't think you can assure me of anything. My mother-in-law is on that plane. Can you assure my wife that her mother will be all right, that the terrorist will not harm her? There are over two hundred people being held hostage, fearing for their lives, and the CIA doesn't even know about it. I don't know how you got this job, but it doesn't look as if you will keep it very much longer. If Joe Campbell speaks to anyone other than federal agents, you and Ray Silva will be holding hands in the unemployment line. Do I make myself clear?"

"Yes, Mr. President."

"Then enjoy the rest of your day and be sure to give Mr. Silva my regards."

Bill Pitts left the Oval Office in a daze. He was not usually that passive, but he had been caught off guard, and he still was not sure what was going on. The only thing he could ascertain from his first encounter with the new President was that an American plane had been hijacked and that the President's mother-in-law was on board. He didn't even know who Joe Campbell was, but figured he had better find out in a hurry. He wondered how the President found out before the heads of the FBI and CIA. It was too late to be concerned with that at this time. He had to find out exactly what had happened and who was responsible.

Dale Patton sat down behind his desk. Someone out there was testing him, trying to humiliate him. On top of everything else, Katherine was right in the middle of it. His wife was strong, but he was not sure if she could handle this. He was about to find out though.

Katie walked through the door of his office. She had received Patton's message of an emergency and could tell by his facial expression that something was seriously wrong.

"What's wrong Dale, what's the emergency? Are we in some sort of danger?"

"No, we aren't, but your mother is. Her plane was hijacked in Cairo."

Katie was stunned; she could not believe what she had just heard. She looked into her husband's eyes and saw very little hope. She started to cry and had a hard time controlling her emotions. This had never been a problem for her in the past. Patton handed her his handkerchief, grabbed her around the shoulders, and guided her to a chair.

Her voice breaking, Katie asked, "Is Mother all right?"

"As far as we know, she is. One of her bodyguards was killed and the other was badly wounded. Therefore, we have to assume whoever is behind this knows who she is."

"You don't know who is responsible for the hijacking?"

"Not yet, but we expect to hear from them soon. I will be leaving for Camp David within the hour, and I want you to come with me. When the media finds out, they will not give you a moment's rest. In fact, they will probably be quite insensitive."

"I'm not concerned about the media. I want to know what you plan on doing about this."

"Calm down, Katie. I will do everything in my power to bring Katherine back safely. I don't like this anymore than you do. You know how I feel about your mom."

"Yes, I do, and that is what concerns me. I know you and Mother don't get along."

General Phillips, Darrin, Bobby, and another Secret Service agent entered the room. They waited at the opposite end of the room to allow the president and first lady to finish their conversation. They could not hear what was being said, but the facial expressions and body language indicated a serious disagreement. Katie turned and left the room. Patton joined the others.

"Air Force One will be Ready in thirty minutes," said Darrin. "I have briefed everyone here on the situation. Tommy asked me to inform you that AWA Flight 454 seems to be heading toward Iraq."

"Iraq", Patton echoed? "That's interesting. How does Tommy get this information so fast?"

"All I know is he made some calls to the Cairo International Airport. How he got this information, and got it so fast, is a mystery to me."

"Connections?" asked Patton.

"Connections," replied Darrin.

"We will be leaving for Camp David in about forty-five minutes. I will set up headquarters there and personally handle this situation. General, you will be coming with me. Contact the Chiefs of Staff and tell them that every branch of the military is on-call 24/7 until further notice. In addition, every branch has to be ready to move large quantities of soldiers and equipment within the next six hours. Darrin, inform John Clermont and Bryce Duncan to meet us at Air Force One. I was scheduled to meet with them briefly tonight anyway."

John Clermont was the secretary of state under the previous administration. Patton really liked him. He had been more productive than anyone else had been in a long time. Bryce Duncan was the secretary of defense. He was competent but rubbed Patton the wrong way. His future in Patton's cabinet had not yet been decided. His behavior and input in this crisis would determine if he had a place in the new Administration.

"Darrin, you stay here and handle things while I am gone. Tell Tommy to keep up the good work and to notify me immediately when we get a confirmed location where the plane sets down. I will also need you to see if the Senate will approve General Phillips as the new chairman of the Joint Chiefs of Staff. There may be a couple of other emergency approvals I will need. Make sure the powers-that-be are informed of this situation. I will probably need some big favors before this is over with. I will stay in touch with you and Tommy. Does anyone have any questions?"

No one said anything, so they were dismissed. Darrin stayed behind to have a few words with the president.

"Are you all right?"

"Yes, why do you ask?"

"Because you're forming a War Council; I hope you don't plan on shooting first and asking questions later?"

"No, but I do plan on getting to the bottom of this very quickly. I think someone is trying to test the new president."

"You're taking this too personally, Mr. President. Don't let your mother-in-law being involved cause you to make a bad decision. You don't have a cabinet formed, and other than Bobby and me, you don't have any advisers you can trust."

"Don't worry, Darrin, I'm under control. The cards have been dealt. Since folding is not an option, I have to play my hand the best way I know how. Who was that other agent that came in with Bobby? I don't know him."

"That is Marty Hickman. He used to head the president's personal security until you requested Bobby. He was probably assigned to you because of his experience. How did Katie take the news?"

"She took it pretty well, considering the circumstances. I am a bit concerned about her, though. That is the first time I can remember seeing her cry. She doesn't want me to take any unnecessary risk, of course, but like you, she doesn't want our personal interest to affect my decision-making. I tried to persuade her to come to Camp David with me to avoid the media. I have never seen her so scared, and I'm afraid the media will make things worse."

"So, what's the verdict?"

"She is staying here."

Forty-five minutes later, the presidential party was boarding Air Force One. Patton entered first, followed by General Phillips. Bryce Duncan and John Clermont were next. Marty and a dozen other Secret Service Agents followed Bobby on board. Everything was very regimented. There was no wasted movement or idle chitchat. Everyone took their seats and buckled up. Air Force One was soon rolling down the runway.

Darrin watched until the plane was out of sight, then he returned to his waiting limousine.

"God help whoever is responsible for this," he said as he returned to the White House.

Patton was quiet and preoccupied. He was preparing himself mentally for a tough fight. The possible losses and sacrifices, which could be inevitable, were going through his mind. He knew how he wanted to proceed, but he had to be sure not one single item was overlooked.

"Mr. President," Clermont said, trying to get the President's attention. "Tommy Granger is on line one."

Patton had been so lost in thought he had not heard the telephone ring. He was anxious to know if Tommy had any more information. He knew he was competent, but he had no idea how much of an asset he was becoming.

"I hope this is good news Tommy," he said after picking up the phone.

"Mr. President, Joe Campbell has regained consciousness and has identified the terrorist leader. His name is Ockbar Shalam; there are five of them in all. The only thing this character said was that he wants his brother released. Joe thought he recognized another man but couldn't recall his name."

"Rahman Mustaffa," said Patton.

"Excuse me, sir?"

"Rahman Mustaffa is probably the other man agent Campbell recognized. Where you find one, you'll likely find the other. Now I know what this is all about. Good work, Tommy; keep me informed," Patton said and then he hung up the phone.

"More bad news, Mr. President," asked John Clermont.

"Actually, it was a bit enlightening. I just found out that Ockbar Shalam is behind the hijacking. He is the most wanted terrorist in the world. Hijacking planes aren't his style; blowing them up maybe, but not hijacking them. Why would he take a plane instead of just blowing it up, like he usually does?"

"I can answer that," interrupted Bobby. "The president led the mission that captured his brother. Ahmed Shalam, who was given the death penalty and is scheduled to be executed next month. He knows who the new president is. My bet is that he's trying to free his brother and humiliate the president at the same time. By the way, he probably will kill everyone on board, like he usually does."

"I'm sure you're right, Bobby. Those probably are his intentions. I just don't think he realizes that he's putting thousands of lives at risk if that happens. Maybe he just doesn't care."

"It sounds as if you're referring to a war, Mr. President," said Clermont. "How can a war be declared on five men? What kind of man are we dealing with?"

Clermont sat back in his chair. At that particular moment, Ockbar Shalam was not the man he was most concerned about.

CHAPTER SEVEN

Senator Dooley sat back in his chair. His fingers were interlocked, with both index fingers pressed together against his lips. Both of his elbows rested on the arms of his chair. His face was not as tense as it had been upon his return from speaking with the President. He had calmed down tremendously, almost as if he had been sedated. At this moment, he was not a Senator, he was a general. He sat upright with perfect posture, plotting, scheming and calculating every detail of his retaliation. As he reached for his cell phone, it rang. Startled, Dooley jerked his hand back. A bit embarrassed, he looked around the room as if someone was watching him. He reached for his cell phone once more.

"Hello," he growled.

"I don't have time to repeat anything, so listen carefully."

Dooley did as he was instructed. The caller had his complete attention. He had called on a private line, one that not even Dooley's secretary had. Only a handful of people had the number to this phone. Dooley listened attentively as he was informed about the hijacking of AWA Flight 454. A smile spread across his face when he was given all the details. The caller was well informed. Although the call only lasted ninety seconds, Dooley now knew as much about the incident as anyone.

"I'll call again when I can."

"Good work! Keep me informed," said Dooley before he turned his phone off and put it in his pocket.

Dooley stood and began to pace the floor. He was already planning how to use this information. He still had that mischievous smile, like a young boy waiting for the bucket of water to fall on your head. He did not get to enjoy the moment very long before his assistant interrupted him.

"This had better be good Rachel."

"Senator, Director Pitts is here to see you."

"Perfect timing, send him in."

Bill Pitts was small compared to Dooley. He stood five feet ten inches tall, weighed 180 pounds, and had no facial hair. He was in his early fifties, wore wire-rim glasses, and combed his hair from one ear to the other around the back of his head. He looked harmless and timid but was actually just the opposite. Pitts had often been linked to organized crime, but it was more rumor than fact; (though as head of the CIA, he had arranged for the disappearance of a person or two).

Pitts was concerned that he had no dirt on Patton, and that could not be right. Nobody became president without dirtying their hands a time or two. The power that Patton commanded, even before he won the election, was a grave concern. This was what was going through his mind when Dooley met him at the door.

"Hello, Nick, how have you been?"

"Nick" was a name only a few people used to refer to Pitts. "Eagle Eye" was the nickname he had acquired at an early age, after a horrible accident left him with a glass left eye. Dooley didn't care much for that nickname, because he didn't think Pitts was as sharp and observant as the name implied. Pitts was well known for cutting himself shaving and always seemed to have a Band-Aid on his face.

While others used the nickname in fun, Dooley used it as a put-down and always emphasized it when he said it.

"Make it quick, Dooley; I'm on my way out."

"I'll be brief. What do you think of the new President?"

"Funny you should ask. I just had an interesting conversation with him about thirty minutes ago."

"Really? About what?"

"It wasn't really a conversation, because he was doing all of the talking. I was getting my ass chewed out about something I should have known about before him. I can't get into that now. What is on your mind?"

"He must have been asking you about the hijacking of AWA flight 454."

"How did you know about that? Don't tell me you had something to do with that plane being taken?"

"No, but I almost wish I did, especially since Patton's mother-in-law is on board."

"What's going on Dooley? What are you up to? Why are you asking me about Patton?"

"Because I don't think he is qualified to be President."

Pitts knew this conversation had nothing to do with Patton's qualifications, which was a moot point now. He searched Dooley's eyes for clarification. He knew exactly where this was heading. Neither man broke eye contact nor said a word for a full minute, but the message was clear.

"You're asking a lot, Pitt finally said." "Do you really hate the man that much?"

"You don't know the half of it."

"That I believe, but why should I help you? He hasn't done anything to me."

"Not yet, he hasn't. This is only his first day in office, and you just told me how he ripped your ass."

"That's not good enough. You're a sore loser, and this sounds like a personal vendetta to me. I don't get involved in people's personal problems. What's in it for me?"

"First of all, you get to keep your job. On his first day in office, he already believes you are incompetent. I know you have noticed how popular the man is. That popularity translates into power, enough power to do whatever he pleases. That includes replacing us if we don't move fast. You were arguably the most powerful man in the world at one time. It seems as if the power structure has shifted over-night. Besides, this wouldn't be the first time you made someone disappear."

"You really need to remember that, especially if you're trying to force my hand. I don't take kindly to blackmail."

"I wouldn't think of it," said Dooley, flashing that mischievous smile. "But you have to admit, things would be a lot better for both of us if Patton wasn't in the picture."

"You're forgetting something. He's the President of the United States, with a very capable personal bodyguard. Every second of the President's coming and going is documented. Second, the vice-president would make a very good President. He and Patton are close friends, which means he would not rest until he dug up the truth. My bet is you would be the first place he would start, and I would be the second."

"Maybe, but the Secretary of State would move up in rank, and he's controllable."

"Let me think about it for a while. Personally, I think this hijacking situation will all but bury him anyway. Those hostages will all be killed, if they're not dead already. That will make the President look like a wimp. He will lose a lot of support, especially since he emphasized in his campaign speeches how he believed in a strong military. I think your problem is taken care of. We can reevaluate the situation at a later date if he lands on his feet."

"I can't take that chance. You don't know this man like I do. He always lands on his feet. This has to be done now, within the week. This is the perfect opportunity, because he is giving all of his attention to the terrorist situation."

"Dooley, you're talking about taking out the President of the United States, not some two-dollar whore with a get-rich-quick scheme. This is not a spur-of-the-moment decision. What's your hurry anyway?"

"It's just that the timing is perfect. Not only is he preoccupied in an international incident, he is headed for Camp David, where we have people that can get to him."

"Then why do you need me? Are you afraid to give the order?"

"You know me better than that. I need you for the cover up, to make sure there are no loose ends. This is what you do, Nick; you're good at it."

"Tying up loose ends only works if there's a well-thought-out, perfectly executed plan. It's not the result of a knee jerk reaction. I'll think about it," Pitts said as he turned and headed for the door.

"I need an answer tonight, one way or the other."

Pitts left the room and gently closed the door behind him. Dooley was in a big hurry to get rid of the President, which meant he had a motive. That could be useful, thought Pitts, especially since he had no serious issues with the President.

Dooley half smiled as he walked over to his desk. He reached for his desk telephone but then decided against it. Sitting in his chair, he pulled his cell phone from his pocket.

"This will be harder to trace."

He dialed a number, punching in a code first, so his number wouldn't show up, and then pulled a handkerchief from his back pocket and placed it over the phone. Dooley leaned back in his chair and propped his feet up on his desk. He was making sure the media knew far more than Patton wanted them to know. He wished he could see their faces at the press conference.

CHAPTER EIGHT

Twenty or thirty members of the press were present as Darrin and Tommy entered the room. Tommy whispered something in the vice president's ear before he approached the microphone. Cameras began to flash as Darrin began to speak.

"Good afternoon, ladies and gentlemen. There are a few events that have taken place in the last few hours, which you should be made aware of. There has been a crime committed against the United States, and the President has decided to handle it personally. In fact, he and a few advisors are on their way to Camp David at this very moment. The President asked me to let you know that with the Senate's approval, General Gary Phillips will be replacing Richard Payne as Commander of the Joint Chiefs of Staff. He also wants you to know that he plans on keeping John Clermont as Secretary of State.

"But Clermont and Phillips are republican," shouted someone from the floor.

"Are they really," mocked Darrin, drawing a few laughs.

"Let's hear about the missing plane," shouted another journalist, which instantly removed the smile from Darrin's face. He locked in on the person behind the voice. He was being tested. She was waiting to catch him in a lie.

"Ladies and gentlemen, Press Secretary Tommy Granger will inform you about the incident in which Miss Mason is most interested. Play it straight," whispered Darrin as he and Tommy exchanged places.

"Ladies and gentlemen we have learned that American World Airlines Flight 454 has been hijacked. There are 212 twelve people on board. The plane is headed in the general direction of Iraq, but since it has not landed, we cannot confirm Iraq as its final destination."

"Excuse me, Mr. Granger," interrupted Michelle Mason, "is it true Ockbar Shalam is responsible for the hijacking?"

Tommy fought the urge to question her about her source of information. That would surely have put him on the defensive. If she knew about Ockbar, she knew about Katherine as well. He had to end this press conference in a hurry.

"He is definitely a suspect," said Tommy, never changing his facial expression. "We have not heard from the perpetrators so we cannot confirm who is responsible or what their reasons are. The President is setting up headquarters at Camp David, and as the vice president said, he will be handling negotiations personally."

"Is that because his mother-in-law is on that plane?"

The journalists hurried to jot down every word between Mason and the Press Secretary.

"No, it's because he considers any attack against citizens as a slap in the face."

"How is the first lady handling the news, especially since she puts such high priority on family values?"

"The first lady is doing well. Of course, she is upset, as anyone would be in this situation. All in all, she is handling the situation very well."

"I heard she has been throwing up since she received the news and is a total wreck."

"Don't believe everything you hear," said Katie, as she entered the room escorted by two Secret Service agents.

Darrin and Tommy both suppressed smiles. They were glad the first lady was up to the challenge. They knew she was not feeling well after the news, but she bought a calming influence to the room.

"I don't know who your sources are Ms. Mason, I only hope you are not paying them for information. Yes, a plane was hijacked, and yes, my mother is on board. There is not any more information we can give you at this time."

Determined to keep the heat on, Michelle continued to probe for information. "I also heard one of your mother's bodyguards was killed. Can you confirm that?"

"Really? Who was killed?"

"I don't have a name but…"

"But your source told you it happened; therefore, it must be so. Ms. Mason, any time this many people are involved in a hostage situation, it's safe to bet a few will be sacrificed by the perpetrators to show they mean business. After all, they are terrorists. It sounds to me as if you are on a fishing expedition. To be a good angler, you have to be patient. Give us some time to verify what it appears your sources already know. We will keep you all informed as this unfolds, but for now, this press conference is over."

Katie turned and walked out of the room. Darrin and Tommy were directly behind her, with the Secret Service bringing up the rear. Members of the media continued to call out questions but the trio never responded. The three of them knew something was terribly wrong. The anchor from Channel 8 knew entirely too much. She was a good investigative reporter and could cause a lot of problems.

Michelle Mason was very popular in the area. Many people considered her reports as the gospel truth. If you got on her bad side it could be very difficult to win a local election. Depending on the issue, she could rival the President himself as the most trusted person in DC, and he was a decorated war hero. She carried a bit of influence on the national scene as well. Six years earlier, she had uncovered a scandal by the popular and respected mayor of DC. He had been convicted of vote tampering and was removed from office. She helped put quite a few power-hungry politicians behind bars. Since then, she has been on the must-hire radar of every major news organization in the country. That's why she loved D.C.; everybody had a skeleton in their closet. All she had to do was dig it up.

"Are you really as calm as you pretend to be," asked Darrin, breaking the silence?

"Hardly," replied Katie, "but I have to be strong for Mother's sake. Tommy, I have to apologize to you for taking over your press conference. That Michelle Mason is a tough cookie, and hopefully my calm appearance in front of the other media people helped take the tension out of the room. Dale and I both think you're doing a great job."

"Thank you Mrs. Patton, no need for apologies. Your timing and demeanor were perfect. If you weren't the first lady I think I would be out of a job."

"Thanks, but no thanks. However, if I make it through this in one piece, I may consider acting as a new career. I need to go to the ladies' room. You two better bring Dale up to speed about the information leak."

Katie put her hands to her mouth and quickly ducked into a nearby restroom. The agents waited outside the door while Darrin and Tommy continued down the hall.

"I wonder where Mason is getting her information from," remarked Darrin.

"I don't know, but she was pretty well informed. Do you think we have a fox in the hen house?"

"That is a good possibility, but it could also be a ploy of the terrorist. They could be feeding the media information to create havoc and turmoil internally. I am glad Katie ended the press conference when she did, before Miss Mason inquired about her security escort. The Secret Service is usually not so visible at these press conferences, and I am sure she would have tried to blow it out of proportion."

"You're right about that. I never thought about the information leak originating from the terrorist camp. I better do as Katie said and give the President a call. You know how he hates surprises."

"In the meantime, I'm going to call Cairo, and see about expediting Joe's trip back here to the states. You did a good job back there, Tommy."

"Thanks, but that Michelle is a character. She tried to set us up, catch us in a lie."

"I'm glad you noticed that. That's why I told you to play it straight. Now you know why she is nicknamed The Lie Detector. She likes to put people on the spot."

"I'm glad Katie came in when she did. She really hurt the credibility of Michelle's source. Our first day on the job has started out with a bang. I wonder what the rest of the year will be like."

"If we make it through the rest of the week, the rest of the year should be a piece of cake. I'll see you in about thirty minutes."

The two men parted company as they headed for their offices. Though things had not gone as smoothly as they would have liked, Tommy had enjoyed every minute of it. He had never fought in a war, but he couldn't come much closer than the hijacking situation. The president was involved, the military was on standby, lives were at stake and he was right in the middle of it all making a positive contribution. He was tingling with excitement as he walked down the hall. He knew he had a ways to go, but he was starting to feel like one of the gang.

Upon reaching his office, Tommy picked up his desk phone and began calling Air Force One. He suddenly stopped and put the receiver back down on its base. The President would not answer the phone while on board, and everyone else with him was a suspect, everyone, that is, except for Bobby Parker. He would call him on his headset.

Bobby had designed the headsets himself, and no one but his men wore them. The headsets could be used as a telephone or as a walkie-talkie. Each headset had its own personal identification number, similar to a telephone number. Bobby could even make a conference call in which all of his men could hear him at the same time. He could include or exclude as many of his men as he wanted. This was a security measure in case any of his men ever went rogue. Bobby could even check all of the calls made or received from each headset, and could distinguish each by person, date, time, and location, much like the public telephone service.

Bobby heard a low humming in his ear. Only his men and a handful of other people had his headset number. Everyone knew it was only to be used for work and during emergency situations, and this call was not coming from one of his men. What was so important that the telephone on the plane was inadequate? He reached down on his belt, to a beeper sized control box, and pressed a button.

"This had better be important," he answered.

"Bobby, this is Tommy. Tell the President that someone is leaking information to the press and that person could be aboard Air Force One."

"Explain," Bobby said, as his eyes slowly surveyed the plane for possible suspects.

"I just finished the press conference and the anchor from Channel 8 knows as much as we do about the hijacking, if not more. She named Ockbar Shalam as the mastermind behind it all. She knows that the President's mother-in-law is on board. She even knows about the shooting of the bodyguards. Darrin and I agree that either the terrorists are purposely feeding the media information to cause more problems, or someone internally is leaking information to discredit and embarrass the new administration. If there is an internal leak, it could just as well be coming from the White House. Keep your eyes and ears open, just in case."

"Isn't Michelle Mason the anchor for Channel 8?"

"Yes, she is."

"Did she say where she got her information?"

"No, she just referred to a source. As we speak, Darrin is trying to speed up plans to have Joe Campbell flown back to Washington."

"Good work. Stay in touch."

"Bobby, one more thing before you leave."

"Go ahead, I'm still with you."

"The first lady made an appearance at the press conference. She held up really well. The president would have been proud of her. She made a timely appearance when Mason was questioning the first lady's mental and physical health. Katie did a good job of discrediting her source, but she ran to the ladies' room, as sick as a dog, when the press conference ended. I hope this isn't one of those situations that drag on for months and months."

"I catch your meaning Tommy. Keep me informed."

Bobby ended the connection by pressing the button on his control box again. He sat back and studied everyone on the plane. He immediately ruled out all of his men. They had been with him for years and he trusted them without question. He was pretty sure he could rule out John Clermont, but everyone else was a suspect. Bobby counted heads as he lifted himself from his seat. Everyone was in plain sight but the president, which worked out well, because he needed to talk to him in private. The president was behind closed doors in his private suite. He was sitting at his desk when he heard the buzzing through the intercom. He looked at his security monitor, saw that it was Bobby, and pressed a button on his desk panel.

"Come on in. The door's open."

Bobby entered the room and closed the door behind him.

"Mr. President, there is something you should be aware of."

"Cut the formalities Bobby, what's going on?"

"I just received a call from Tommy. It seems that someone is leaking information to the media."

"What did he say?"

"He just finished his press conference, and the anchor from Channel 8, Michelle Mason, knew as much about the hijacking as we do. She knows that Katherine is on the plane and that Ockbar Shalam is involved."

"There goes our media blackout. Did she say how she obtained this information?"

"Not specifically. She just said something about a source. It could be almost anyone. The lead could even be originating from the terrorists themselves. I will vouch for all of my men."

"Get Tommy back on the phone. I want complete background checks of everyone on this plane, other than your men. I want information on everyone at Camp David, including Secret Service. Get

Darrin to pull an updated profile on Ockbar Shalam. I need this done ASAP, preferably by the time we land. Since we don't know who we can trust, remind Darrin to be extremely cautious who he talks to."

"Exactly what will they be looking for?"

"I would start with Dooley and anyone who has worked for him, served under him, or owes him a favor. Next would be Richard Payne, though I am not sure how much he knows, and anyone else of high rank that feels their job is at risk. I want you to stay on top of this Bobby."

"I'm on it. Tommy also mentioned that Darrin was speeding up the return of Joe Campbell, and that Katie did an excellent job in discrediting Mason's source. He said Katie appeared strong and confident in front of the cameras but is actually taking this pretty hard. Tommy doesn't know how long she can hold up."

"Understood, but I don't plan on this going on for too long. Ask Clermont to step back here for a few minutes. We need to contact the Iraqi government to see if they will help if the plane lands there."

"Do you really expect them to?"

"No, but I have to ask. That's protocol, you know. My response to this hijacking will depend on where the plane lands and if that country will aid us in this matter, or at least not tie our hands. If the country refuses to help us, we could be in the middle of another war. That reminds me, I need to see if congress will allow me to classify this as an act of war if it comes to that."

CHAPTER NINE

Everyone aboard the hijacked plane was lost in thought, wondering what the future would bring. The flight had been fairly smooth, except for an occasional air pocket. The pilot glanced over at his injured co-pilot. The left side of his face was swollen and had turned purple. Blood still trickled from the gash on his cheek, and his left eye was just a slit. The wound needed to be cleaned and stitched, but medical attention was not expected any time soon.

The terrorists had discarded their ground crew uniforms, reverting to their Middle-Eastern attire. This made them appear even more threatening. Ockbar walked over to Ruth and pulled her from her seat. He was not interested in her; it was Katherine he wanted to speak to. He snatched Katherine from her seat in a similar manner and headed down the aisle, almost dragging her to the rear of the plane. He threw her in an empty seat and sat down beside her.

"Please don't hurt her, pleaded Ruth. "She doesn't mean any harm."

One of the terrorists shoved Ruth back down in her seat.

"Rahman, if she speaks again, kill her," ordered Ockbar.

Rahman Mustaffa was second in command and was as cold and heartless as Ockbar. They had worked together many times. Either would kill on a dare. Ruth settled back in her seat and remained as quiet as she could. This man was looking for a reason to hurt her, and she was not going to give him one. She prayed Katherine would be more cooperative and sensible than she had been earlier.

Katherine gathered herself and sat upright. She was terrified but determined not to let it show. "Does that make you feel better," she asked?

As long as she kept talking, she was all right. Her fear seemed to ease as long as she kept a conversation going on with this murderer. As ironic as that was, she realized it was true. These people fed off of fear, and that was exactly what she could not give them. She enjoyed the verbal sparring. As often as she and Dale went at it, she realized this was something she did well. She reminded herself that this man was not Dale; she had to be careful not to push him too far. Her head was clearer when she was talking. The waiting and wondering unnerved her.

"Who are you," Ockbar asked, challenging her with his eyes.

Katherine calmly turned her head and looked out the window. Ockbar grabbed her chin and turned her face until they made eye contact once more.

"I will ask you once more, who are you?"

"My name is Katherine Morrison," she said in a strong, steady voice.

"Why does Katherine Morrison have two bodyguards?"

Katherine hesitated for a moment but realized this was not the time to be obstinate. She remembered him asking Joe about his standard issue firearm and figured he already had an inkling of who she might be. She did, however, decide to see how much he knew about her son-in-law.

"Dale Patton is my son," she said, accepting his challenge and issuing one of her own.

Ockbar maintained the eye contact, searching her face for the truth. Katherine never blinked or looked away, using every ounce of courage she had. A wide smile spread across his face. He apparently did not know that the President's parents were deceased, but he obviously did know who Dale Patton was.

"Excellent," said Ockbar, "and who is your traveling companion?"

"She is my personal assistant."

"This is better than I ever imagined. I have the mother of the president of the United States in my possession. I must be living right."

"Why are you doing this?"

"Do not worry Katherine Morrison, you will be made aware of everything in due time. In fact, you will be my special guest. In the meantime, go back to your seat and buckle up. We are about to land."

Katherine was escorted back to her seat. Ockbar was not as rough as he had been moments earlier. Maybe this was a good sign. She knew she had put herself right in the middle of whatever it was he had planned. She just hoped no one else would be hurt. Since he had the president's mother, maybe he would release the others.

"What was that little chat about," Ruth asked, as Katherine sat down and strapped herself in.

"He wanted to know who we were since we were traveling with two bodyguards."

"Did you tell him who you were?"

"I had to; I had no choice. He suspected something anyway, after he discovered Joe and Charlie were Secret Service. Don't worry Ruth; they won't dare harm the mother and aunt of the president of the United States."

Ruth's mouth plopped open in disbelief. She reached in her purse and pulled out a pill bottle. She quickly uncapped it and popped two little blue pills in her mouth. She closed the bottle and then settled back in her seat and closed her eyes. The plane began to descend.

Ockbar was in the cockpit, talking on the radio, when the plane made its approach. He was getting instructions from someone. The pilot could tell they were landing on a runway, but it was not a commercial runway. They were landing at a military airfield. From his instruments, the pilot figured they were a good deal south of Baghdad. When the plane touched down, he was instructed to head toward a large hangar. Upon reaching it, Iraqi soldiers guided the plane inside. The hangar doors closed and the engines were cut off. The pilot and co-pilot were ordered out of the cockpit and were seated with the rest of the passengers.

Ockbar left the plane while the other terrorists stayed on board. Looking out of the windows, the passengers could see very little. The hangar was very dimly lit, and a few soldiers would walk by every so often. Two Iraqi soldiers met Ockbar when he reached the bottom of the steps. Some of the passengers watched them as they talked for a moment and then left the hangar through a door almost directly across from their windows.

"Relax," instructed Rahman from the front of the plane. "You have had a very long night. There are only a few hours until daylight, and tomorrow brings more surprises. On the other hand, some of you might want to stay awake. You might not want to sleep away your last few hours."

Laughing, Rahman opened the door of the plane and said something to the soldiers. Moments later, four soldiers entered the plane, replacing the terrorists who had been on board. Stopping in the doorway, Rahman looked into the faces of the passengers before he departed. Finding what he was looking for, expressions of fear on everyone's face, he released a wicked laugh and slammed the door shut behind him.

The Iraqi soldiers went straight to work. One stayed in the front of the plane while the other three made their way down the aisles. One soldier checked the cockpit to make sure no one was inside. When they were satisfied everyone was in sight, they placed themselves strategically throughout the plane. One soldier stayed in the front of the plane, a second stayed in the rear, and the other two patrolled the aisles.

Ockbar and his four escorts left the hangar and entered a small building about twenty yards away. The outside of it resembled platoon barracks. The inside had been remodeled. There was a wooden table inside the door on the right. At the table were two wooden chairs without padding. Directly behind the table was a hallway with two rooms on each side. The first room on the left was a large empty room. The door was made of large metal bars that contained a padlock. The second room on the left was half as big, with a solid wooden door. The two rooms on the right were of equal size, with hollow wooden doors. The first room on the right was a kitchen complete with stove, sink, refrigerator, and table with matching chairs. The second room on the right was part living quarters, part warehouse. At the end of the hallway was a complete bathroom with commodes, urinals, and a shower stall, but there was no door attached to the rusty hinges. In the back right-hand corner of the building was another wooden door that led outside the building. There were two windows in each room on the right and a small window in the front door. The two rooms on the left had no windows. A concrete floor ran through the entire building.

As Ockbar entered the living quarters, two other men greeted him. They were dressed as soldiers as well. They were wearing military fatigues and shiny black boots, and both of them had pistols holstered on their belts. Like Ockbar, they wore black berets. They were all of medium build and stood about five-feet nine inches tall. Ockbar had a couple of inches on the others.

The two men had been sitting at a table in the left-hand corner of the room. A telephone and a deck of playing cards were the only thing on the table. To the right of the table was a double-sized bed. At the foot of the bed was a makeshift table that contained a small television. A long extension cord ran from the television, under the bed, to an outlet behind the headboard. The right-hand side of the large room was filled with military supplies. There were boxes of boots and extra uniforms, canteens, canned goods, compasses and knives but, the majority of the boxes contained weapons and explosives. There were pistols, rifles, hand grenades, ammunition, dynamite, ignition caps, timers, plastic explosives, and almost any other kind of weapon you can imagine. They were stacked in four neat rows, from the floor to the ceiling, with a narrow walkway between each row.

Ockbar smiled as he stretched out across the bed. He began telling his comrades of his good fortune. With the mother of the president in his possession, he was sure to get a lot of media coverage. His men were very attentive and clung to every word that came from his mouth. He spoke of success, riches, and global fear. Ockbar spoke for about thirty minutes and then ordered them to leave and get some rest. They had only a few hours before phase two would be implemented.

Katherine and Ruth were restless, as were the rest of the hostages. They could not forget Rahman's last statement. Were some of them really going to die in the morning? Maybe this was another scare tactic to keep them under control. The only sounds they heard were those of the boots of the patrolling terrorist, and the squeaking seats of the scared and squirming passengers. Whatever happened the next morning, Katherine knew she could not show signs of fear. She knew she would be the tool Ockbar would use to try to force Patton's hand. She also realized her chances of surviving this ordeal were very slim, especially when he discovered the truth.

Katherine decided to come clean with Ruth before anything happened to either of them. She did not want Ruth to think she had put her life in danger. After the soldier walked past them on his latest round, Katherine nudged her friend and whispered, "Ruth, are you awake?"

"Isn't everybody," she replied?

"There is something I have to tell you, in case something happens to me."

"Well, whatever happens to you will also happen to me. You made sure of that."

"That's not necessarily true. That's what I want to explain. I lied to you when I said that I had told that jerk you were the president's aunt."

"You didn't tell him that? What did you tell him?"

"I did tell him that I was the president's mother, but I told him you were my personal assistant, not my sister. I knew if I said you were a friend or relative you would be in as much danger as I am. I don't want anyone else to die because of me. I made myself the center of attention, praying no one else would be injured."

"Katherine, I ... I don't know what to say."

"Don't say anything. If you do, I will probably start to cry, and I can't let them see me break down like that. Just remember that there is a method to the madness of everything I do and say from here on out."

The terrorist was walking back up the aisle, getting close to Katherine and Ruth. They turned their heads slightly away from each other and closed their eyes until he had passed.

"You have to remember that you are my assistant, and you have to go along with whatever I might do. Now get some rest." Katherine leaned her head back, rested it on the back of her seat and closed her eyes.

Ruth wanted to console her longtime friend, but she dared not say anything more. She could see that Katherine was struggling to maintain control of her emotions. She was not the same sarcastic, self-centered person who boarded the plane. Katherine was trying to be strong. The no nonsense, leadership attitude she was exhibiting was impressive. Ruth did not know what to say or how to comfort her friend. She turned her head away from Katherine. The tears coming down her cheeks would just upset her even more. As hard as it was to sleep before, now it would be impossible.

It seemed like only minutes had passed since Katherine had closed her eyes. Just when she was starting to settle down and relax, the slamming of the aircraft door startled her and the other hostages. Two more terrorists had just entered the plane. They looked around, as if searching for someone. As they headed down the aisle, everyone looked away, refusing to make eye contact. Katherine was sure they were coming for her, but they walked right past her. One terrorist stopped by a little old lady and smiled. He said something in Arabic to his buddy, and they shared a laugh.

"You come with me," said the terrorist, pointing at the little old lady.

Frightened, the elderly woman began to cry and clutched her husband's arm. Expecting the worse, the old man's eyes began to fill with tears as well.

"Let my wife stay here," pleaded the old man, "I will go with you. Take me instead."

"Maybe next time," said the terrorist, pulling the woman from her husband's grasp.

The old man held on as long as he could, but his strength was not what it once was. He jumped up to follow his wife but was easily pushed back into his seat. The woman sobbed hysterically as she was taken from the plane.

The hangar doors were open, allowing the morning sunlight to enter. Ockbar, Rahman, and five other terrorists could be seen. One of the terrorists was setting up a camera on a tripod. As Ockbar barked orders, everyone moved into place. The one terrorist almost dragged the little old lady to the spot where he wanted her. They were right below the windows of the aircraft. The camera and its operator were right in front of them, about twenty feet away. Ockbar was also in front of the camera, about ten feet away and a little to the left.

Through his lens, the camera operator made sure he could see Ockbar, the old lady, and the hostages peering through the windows of the plane. A few other terrorists had surrounded the little old lady, and all of them were included in the cameraman's shot.

"What are they going to do?"

Everybody on that side of the plane, including Katherine and Ruth, began watching the spectacle. People who had been seated on the opposite side of the plane stood up and stretched their necks in an attempt to see what was happening. Some went over to the opposite side of the plane and peered over the shoulders of those seated to get a better view. The Terrorists forced everyone to return to their assigned seat, except for the woman's husband.

The red light on the camera signaled that it was now recording. For the first few minutes, the camera was focused on Ockbar. The hostages knew he was speaking but could not hear his voice. The camera operator slowly refocused his lens to pick up the old lady, and the terrorist next to her who suddenly cocked back his right hand and struck the tiny woman in the temple. She crumbled like a dry leaf, dead before she hit the ground. Adding insult to injury, the terrorist withdrew his pistol and fired off two rounds into her lifeless body.

"Nooooo, noooo, stop," screamed the woman's husband.

That entire side of the plane, and a few standing hostages on the opposite side, witnessed the execution. They were crying and screaming as the camera recorded their reactions. Their outburst triggered the same response from the opposite side of the plane. Most of the hostages on the opposite side of the plane did not witness the execution, but they heard the gunshots, and their imagination filled in the blanks. They were all hysterical, and only more threats of violence brought them under control. Still filming, the camera operator had zoomed in on the execution and the reaction of the hostages. He filmed a few moments longer, going back and forth from the small, lifeless body to the terror and fear that was evident on the faces of the hostages. Turning the camera off, the camera operator walked over to Ockbar.

"Make the necessary adjustments and then send a copy of the tape to the media," ordered Ockbar. "As far as the old lady is concerned, leave her there for a couple of hours in plain view of her comrades, and then put her in a box behind the building. We will have a pile of bodies to torch before this is all over."

Ockbar walked toward the plane, followed by Rahman. They climbed the steps and entered the plane. The little old lady's husband jumped from his seat and headed straight toward the terrorist leader. He was intercepted by one of Ockbar's men, who pushed him to the floor. The old man got up and charged again. This time, the terrorist punched him in the face. The old man struggled to his feet and slowly continued up the aisle. The terrorist pulled his pistol.

"No," shouted Katherine, racing to the old man's side. "Don't you think there has been enough killing for one day?"

"Maybe, maybe not," replied Ockbar. "That depends on your son. If my demands are met, you will all be released. If not, you will all die. If there are any more foolish acts, like the one we just witnessed, you will die slowly and painfully. Not only will that individual die, he or she will determine the deaths of two others. I hope I make myself clear, because no form of disobedience will be tolerated."

"You have me," said Katherine, "which is more than you had planned. I am the only hostage you need. Let the others go."

"On the contrary, I need all of you. I do not believe the president will be convinced by my first production. It will probably only anger him. A larger, more convincing production might be necessary. Do not worry Katherine Morrison; you will get your chance to show your bravery. If you care anything about that old man, you should help him back to his seat before I call my cameraman back."

"Come on, sir," said Katherine, "let me help you. It's not going to do anyone any good if you get yourself killed as well. I bet you have kids and grandkids waiting for you back home."

Sore and bruised, the old man gave in. He allowed Katherine to help him back to his seat as the terrorist holstered his pistol. Katherine returned to her seat. Silently, the old man continued to weep, the tears streaming down his face. Everyone focused their attention on Ockbar. They wondered what other surprises he had in store for them. They did not have to wonder for long.

"Ration whatever food is left on this plane," he ordered his men. "When that is gone, they are to be given only crackers and water. Restroom privileges will be allowed every six hours. The lights on the plane will remain on at all times. Is that understood?"

"As you wish," answered the terrorist who had floored the old man."

Ockbar and Rahman turned and left the plane. As the hostages at the windows watched them walk down the steps, something else caught their attention. The corpse of the tiny old lady was still very much visible.

CHAPTER TEN

B obby and Patton were in the President's personal suite, which was more private and more secure. Patton was on the telephone with Darrin. He was receiving the information he had been waiting on. This information would determine how he would officially respond to the hijacking.

Iraq's answer was just as Patton had anticipated. They would not help in any way to retrieve the American plane that had been taken, refusing even to discuss the situation.

"That is pretty much what I expected," said Patton. "Did the Prime Minister say why he did not want to speak with Clermont?"

"No. I only have a theory Mr. President, Darrin said, "and I am sure you know exactly what I am talking about. He said he would only speak to you. On top of that, the Prime Minister emphasized that any rescue attempt would be considered a hostile act of aggression. His exact quote was "Iraq will protect itself from any hostile act with the full force of its military and its allies."

"He mentioned allies?"

"He most certainly did. It sounds like they are prepared for war."

"It certainly sounds that way, doesn't it? Did our friends from the east have anything else to say?"

"That was it. The Prime Minister kept his reply short and to the point."

"You would think we would get more gratitude than that after ridding their country of bin Laden and breaking up the al-Qaida stronghold. I guess we will hear from the pessimists in congress who were against the withdrawal of all troops from Iraq."

"Don't be concerned with that Dale. Everything President Obama did was criticized and ridiculed as being the wrong thing. We both know he did the right thing. Soldiers being present would not have changed anything. It would have just put them in harm's way."

"That's not a big concern of mine Darrin. I was just thinking out loud. We need congress to declare this as an act of war. I will have Clermont get on that right away. What information do you have on Ockbar and the plane?"

"Ockbar Shalam, as you know, is the most feared terrorist since bin Laden. He is the prime suspect in dozens of terrorist bombings all over the world."

"Skip the resume, Darrin, I need a character profile."

"The CIA files have him listed as NUMB. This is as bad as it gets. He has no conscience. He will kill to entertain himself. One account of Ockbar has him killing a man simply because he was bored and had not killed anyone in over a week. He means what he says and will do exactly what he says he will do. The man loves to be provoked so he can make good on his threats. He is a true terrorist in every sense of the word. By the way, he has never returned a hostage alive."

"It doesn't sound as if those passengers have much of a chance."

"I would assume they are already dead. I think that would be your best approach in this situation."

"I agree, Patton said.

"One last thing, Mr. President, the plane landed south of Baghdad, about fifty miles southwest of Karbala. The Israeli Air Traffic Controllers could not be certain of the exact location because their radar lost connection with the plane in that general location. Their radars are capable of tracking commercial flights one hundred miles farther than where the signal went dead. They may be using some sort of signal-jamming device, or possibly they crashed. There is an old military airport out there somewhere in the desert. Ten to one, that's where you will find our plane."

"I know the area."

"What about the news leak," asked Bobby?"

"Darrin, have you figured out who is leaking information?"

"No, I haven't. Everyone on Air Force One and at Camp David has ties to Dooley, except Bobby's men. I think you can rule out John Clermont and General Phillips. The others should be watched. Most of the officers at Camp David served under Dooley. You and I both know that Dooley wasn't the most-loved person in the service. I am sure there are some there who dislike him as much as we do. On the other hand, there are probably a few there who think he can walk on water. The problem is, I cannot distinguish between them based on their service record. Tell Bobby he has his work cut out for him."

"I think he has already figured that much out. Thanks for the information. Iraq's response pretty much confirms what I had believed from the start, except for the part about allies. It looks like Iraq is aiding and financing Ockbar Shalam. Tell Tommy I will issue a statement later tonight in which he can pass on to the media."

"I'll give him the message Mr. President. Stay in touch."

"What did he have to say about the leak?" asked Bobby, as the President replaced the receiver on its base.

"He said that everybody is a suspect except for your men, Clermont, and General Phillips. He also said that most of the officers here on base have served under Dooley. He feels that some of them can be trusted, but can't tell the good guys from the bad guys by their service records."

"Are you ready to join the party?" asked Bobby. "Everyone is waiting for you."

"Let's not keep them waiting. It looks as if we have another battle with Iraq on our hands. I promise you, this one will not be anything like the Gulf War."

They left the President's personal suite and were instantly greeted by a couple of military policemen. Some of Bobby's men were a few feet down the hall. Bobby always kept his men close by, no matter what other security was present. Bobby and the President turned the corner and were greeted by more military police patrolling the halls. Marty Hickman and a couple of his men were also in the hall, near the entrance of the meeting room.

The room was rectangular, thirty feet by fifty feet. They had entered from one end and looked out over the length of the room. The far wall at the other end of the room contained the presidential seal, which was six feet in diameter. Directly in front of them was a solid oak table with a marble top. The table formed a perfect pentagon, with each side measuring nine feet. It had the presidential seal in the middle of it and had fifteen brown, plush leather chairs around it. General Phillips, John Clermont, and Bryce Duncan were all seated at the end closest to door.

The wall to the right held a large map of the Middle East, Iraq and her neighbors, to be specific. The wall to their left contained a large computerized control panel. It ran the entire length of the wall and was divided into seven sections. Each section contained a copper-colored metal chair with brown leather padding on the seat, back, and armrest. Each seat at the table and each section of the wall length panel had access to a telephone. The double doors they entered were made of solid oak. Two heavily armed guards were always stationed outside those doors.

Marty Hickman and Keith Turner were standing guard inside the room with their backs to these doors. In the corner to the President's immediate right was another paneled station. This station was much smaller and a control panel and a telephone on the wall. This was Bobby's station. The President's seat was located directly in front of this station.

"Hello gentlemen," Patton said as he sat down. "I apologize for taking you away from your families on such short notice. I hope to return you to your loved ones in a matter of days."

Everyone at the table made eye contact after the President's statement. They all figured this would be a long, drawn out affair. Either the President knew something they did not, or this man did not have a clue of the severity of the matter.

"All of you know why we are here," continued Patton, "so let's get to work. We know the plane has landed in Iraq, and we know approximately where it has set down. I have also been informed that Iraq refuses to work with us in retrieving AWA Flight 454. Not only have they refused to help, they said any attempt to rescue the hostages or set foot on Iraqi soil without permission will be considered an act of aggression and will be met with retaliation."

"This is to be expected Mr. President," said General Phillips. "I have a team of the world's finest ready to go in as soon as you give the word."

"I am pleased to know that you already have a plan and a team assembled, General, but I am going to take a different approach. I am not going to send in a handful of troops on a covert mission, at least not yet. I am going to use the strength of the entire military."

Everyone at the table looked at the president in disbelief. They realized this would mean a direct attack against Iraq and another Gulf War.

"How can you justify that?" asked Duncan. "You have no proof that Iraq is behind this. You can't hold the entire country responsible for the actions of a few terrorists. Even if Iraq is behind this, there has to be some type of progressive discipline, which would start with negotiations or sanctions. If that fails, then maybe our actions would progress into retaliation."

"I disagree," said the President. "First of all, I don't negotiate with terrorist. Second, I don't negotiate with anyone to give me back something they've taken from me. Third, the Iraqi government has already refused to help us and has threatened military retaliation. Take into consideration that is a threat just from our inquiry, not from any action. Fourth, there is no way an unauthorized aircraft can enter Iraq's airspace without being detected, especially not a big commercial plane. Therefore, they allowed that plane to enter and to land. Should I continue counting?"

"I agree with Bryce," said General Phillips. "You are most likely 100 percent correct, but we still can't attack Iraq on a hunch. We have no hard evidence."

"We can, and we will, if necessary. I hope to have all the evidence I need by that time. The fact that Iraq allowed the plane to pass through their airspace and land in a remote area is proof enough for me. However, I will get you your evidence. Part of their success depends on us following the talk-first protocol we have always followed in the past."

At that moment, the telephone at Bobby's station rang. It was Tommy. Bobby listened intently for a minute then hung up the phone. He took a deep breath before he said anything.

"Excuse me, Mr. President, there is a breaking story being broadcast that you should see."

Bobby started pressing buttons on the panel. The large map drew up into its casing. Two wooden panels opened, revealing a large flat-screen television. Bobby tuned into the Channel 8 news from DC, where Michelle Mason was reporting the story.

"Ladies and gentlemen, I am Michelle Mason bringing you a Channel 8 News exclusive. We interrupt your regular programming to update you on the hijacking of AWA Flight 454. About an hour ago, via the Internet, we received a tape from hijackers. I must warn you; this is very graphic and is not suitable for young children."

As the tape rolled, everyone in the room glanced back and forth between the TV and the President. Patton's eyes stayed focused on the screen. He showed no signs of emotion. Bobby had seen this expression on numerous occasions. It was the President's poker face, the one he always carried into battle.

"Hello, Mr. President. I am Ockbar Shalam, and as you already know I have your aircraft and all of its passengers. Imagine how pleased I was when I discovered your mother was on board. I did not realize she was a passenger on this plane. I guess I just got lucky. If my brother Ahmed is not delivered to the American Embassy in Baghdad within three days, everyone on this plane will suffer. It is said a picture is worth a thousand words. Let me show you what I mean."

The camera panned over to the little old lady standing next to the terrorist. Her execution, along with the fear on the faces of the remaining hostages, was shown. Ockbar's voice could be heard over the screaming and crying of the passengers.

"That saying has a lot of truth in it. Any rescue attempts will cause more deaths. The treatment this old lady received will be nothing compared to what will happen to your mother if I do not see my brother in three days. You have until noon, your time, to reply or more passengers will die. Mr. President, you will deliver your answer personally on your noonday news. I want your entire country to see the weakling they chose as their leader. I want them to know they will never be safe as long as you are in office. That, my friend, is a promise. If you refuse, two people will die every hour until you show your face. If I run out of bodies before I get my brother, your citizens will perish on their own soil until Ahmed is returned. Good-bye for now; see you on the news."

The tape rolled a few moments longer, showing the body of the dead woman and the screaming and crying of the hostages. The tape went black, and Michele Mason returned.

"Ladies and gentlemen, that was Ockbar Shalam, the most wanted criminal in the world. As you could see, he is responsible for the hijacking of AWA Flight 454, which we reported exclusively earlier this evening. We do not know the identity of the woman who was so brutally murdered, but we will give you that information as soon as we have it. To our knowledge, there have been only two fatalities thus far. A Secret Service Agent was the first person killed and another was wounded. Apparently, the terrorists do not know that the president's mother died years ago. However, our sources have informed us that the president's mother-in-law is on that plane. That's who we believe is the person who has been mistaken for the president's mother. We hope to be able to carry the President's response to you live tomorrow at noon. We have not heard from the White House, so we do not know how this will be handled. Stay tuned, we will return with more coverage of the hijacking of AWA Flight 454."

Bobby turned off the television set. As if it had been rehearsed, everyone turned toward the president to get his response. To their surprise, he was still expressionless. He did not appear to be upset, just in deep thought. The silence was broken when Bobby walked over to Patton and handed him the cordless phone.

"Sir, the vice president would like to speak to you."

"Yes Darrin," answered the President.

"You realize everyone on that plane will be killed, especially Katherine. The media has already identified her as your mother-in-law. That bastard will try to make an example of her when he finds out. Forgive me, Dale, but your mother-in-law has a real talent for getting under people's skin."

"True, but she probably played it better than even she realizes."

"How so?"

"Whether the mother or mother-in-law, Katherine has become his ace in the hole. He probably does plan on killing her and everyone else eventually, but remember, he is a terrorist. The best way for him to get at me is to have my wife and I watch Katherine suffer. Watching someone continuously tortured is harder than knowing they are dead. Katherine may have bought herself more time, but it will most likely be very painful. She will probably wish she was dead before he finishes with her. Katherine's only chance is for us to turn the tables on him."

"How will we do that," said Darrin.

"We have to cause him internal problems like those he is causing us. The killing of Katherine will secure his place in history. He could even become the next Saddam Hussein. Hopefully, Iraq is not ready for that."

"I see where you're going now. It does appear that Iraq is backing this operation. We just have to put a bug in the ear of the right people."

"Yes, along with some military reinforcement. We have no control over Katherine. We just have to pray for the best for her, as well as the others. However, another chat with the Prime Minister could be very interesting."

"It could be at that."

"Don't call him until after I respond at noon tomorrow. On second thought, that is Clermont's territory. I will have him contact the Prime Minister. I want you to get me proof of Iraq's involvement in this mess."

"I just pray to God that Katherine survives, because Katie is having a hell of a time with this. The media has been going crazy trying to get a statement from you. They are wearing poor Tommy out, but he's holding up pretty well. Do you have any idea how you're going to approach this?"

"I know exactly how I am going to handle this. We will hold Iraq responsible and put pressure on them. That's why I need concrete proof that they are behind all this."

"I'll do my best, but it's not going to be easy."

"It never is, Darrin; it never is. Tell Tommy to inform the media that I will issue a transcript of my response about an hour before I go live. I will broadcast from here; only the top ten media outlets in the world will be allowed in. They will have to transfer the broadcast to their affiliates and any other media outlet that wants it live. Also have Tommy go through the FCC and mandate that any other tapes or communication of any type, received from Ockbar Shalam or anyone involving this issue, be delivered to us immediately and not broadcast without my approval. I consider this a national security matter; they will be shut down if they don't comply."

"I'm on it. By the way, I plan to be there before you go live at noon tomorrow. I will see you after you respond to Shalam," said Darrin, right before he pressed the off button.

The President turned the phone off and handed it back to Bobby. Bobby took the phone and returned to his station. Patton redirected his attention back to the people at the table. They realized they were not going to be able to change his mind.

"Well, gentlemen, let's get to work. Bryce, I want you and General Phillips to coordinate the placing of men around the borders of Iraq."

"The entire country," asked Bryce? "That's not possible."

"Are you fighting me, Duncan?"

"No, Mr. President, but..."

"This will be done my way. If you are not with me, you are against me and wasting my time, which I have very little of right now."

"That is not the case at all, sir. I was referring to the opposition from the bordering countries."

"Hear me out Duncan. I realize that not everyone is going to allow us to occupy their land along the Iraqi border. Some will and some won't. While you and the general are routing our forces in the general direction of Iraq, Clermont will be on the horn trying to get permission from those countries to occupy their airspace as well as their borders. Therefore, the three of you must stay in constant contact with each other over the next three days."

"Mr. President," asked General Phillips, "is this going to be another Gulf War?"

"No General. I want as much, if not more, military firepower over there, but it will be fought differently. First, I want to maintain air superiority at all times. Once we control the skies, we will not allow any planes to leave the ground, military or civilian. Our ground crew will be there to keep any high-ranking officials from sneaking out of the country."

"Are you talking about shooting down civilian planes, sir?"

"No, any commercial planes that are airborne will be forced to land back in Iraq. However, I am prepared to destroy the commercial airports as well as the ones on military bases if I have to. If necessary, we will attack with long-range missiles and bombers, but our F-15s will do most of the damage. I don't want any hand-to-hand combat unless it is forced on us. In essence, gentlemen, it will be target practice. I want all of our big guns in the area. Our bombers, battle ships, and aircraft carriers, I want them all over there."

"How long will we keep this up," asked General Phillips? "What if Iraq still denies involvement?"

"This won't last long. Ockbar gave me three days to return his brother; I am going to give them the same three days to return our plane."

"Or else?"

"Or, depending on the evidence we have at that time, it could mean a full out attack against Iraq. Which means one way or another, this should all be over within a week. Just to be on the safe side, Clermont will contact the American Embassy in Iraq and have all Americans start evacuating immediately."

"What if we can't produce the proof we need against Iraq," asked General Phillips?

"I haven't figured that one out yet. None of you have to worry about that, because you are only following orders. You can blame everything on the crazy new president. It is time to get to work. I want status reports from each of you every hour. I want 70 percent of those we deploy to be in place by the time I go on the air tomorrow. I want to start taking control of the Iraqi airspace at exactly the same moment I go on air. No one talks to the press but me, Tommy, or Darrin. You are dismissed, if there are no more questions."

Everyone stood up and began to exit the room. Bryce Duncan parted his lips, gestured with his left hand, and started to speak. He changed his mind, closed his eyes, and began massaging his temples.

He picked up his brief case and proceeded out of the double doors.

CHAPTER ELEVEN

The media had arrived. Hundreds of journalists, photographers and camera crews had descended upon Camp David. News trucks, with their call letters on the side, were lined up as far as the eye could see. Mounted cameras and satellite feeds had sprung up like wild dandelions and surrounded the perimeter of the compound. Journalists were literally fighting to get the best position for their shots. Only the select few were allowed inside the compound. The rest were lined along the perimeter battling to maintain or improve their position.

"The show has officially started," said Bobby as he looked out the window. "This is the largest and most dangerous media circus I have ever been involved with. It is a security nightmare."

"Relax Bobby, Patton said. "Everybody is here; the Secret Service, the FBI, the CIA and no telling how many of your men you have roaming around. I have more bodyguards than you can keep up with. I'll be fine."

"That is exactly the problem," emphasized Bobby as he turned to face the President. "The FBI and CIA are not on security detail and I don't trust either of them at this time, especially the CIA, with the history Dooley has with Pitts. Have you forgotten that Dooley is here in the compound? You gave him until the end of the week to leave Washington, remember?"

"No, I haven't forgotten, and I meant it. Dooley's not stupid; he knows we will be watching him."

"He may not be stupid, but he is desperate, and that's worse."

"Why is he here anyway?" asked the President. "And how did he get clearance to get in here?"

"He is still a senator, so getting in here would not have been a problem. However, he is here with the media. He is a guest of Ms. Mason. She will be hosting a spot before you go on the air and Dooley is her special guest. She will be asking him why he is not one of your confidants, since the two of you have worked together before on terrorist activities. Of course, the good senator will be telling the world how incompetent you are, and how he was the brains behind all of your glory."

"I must watch that. It should be interesting."

"You won't have to wait much longer. It is due to air in about thirty-five minutes. How is the troop positioning going?"

"Good question, because I am not exactly sure. One minute we seem to have approval, and the next it seems that the country has changed its mind or needs more time before they can give us an answer. Iran and Turkey have given us a definite no, and the other countries seem to be on the fence."

"I would have thought Iran would have been the first to cooperate, as much friction as there has been between Iran and Iraq over the years."

"I guess their distrust of the United States outweighs their hatred for Iraq. I sense something more is going on. This may play out bigger than even I thought."

"Have you have considered the possibility that Iran and Iraq are joining forces? Never mind, don't answer that. It was a stupid question."

"It wasn't a stupid question, and yes, I have considered it. It seems that more than just Iran could be coming to Iraq's aide. That is my biggest concern at this point. I had not planned on that but will be ready if it does happen."

Bobby returned to the window and continued to observe the masses. In less than ninety minutes, the president would give Ockbar his reply. Patton was feeling a bit uneasy about his predicament. He could not remember the last time he felt this way about a decision he had made. Then again, he had never been in a situation in which the death of a family member would probably be blamed on him.

"Hello, I am Michelle Mason and I'd like to welcome you to this special report on the hijacking of AWA Flight 454."

Michelle was sitting in a padded chair with Senator Dooley sitting to her right. The set resembled that of a talk show.

"AWA Flight 454 was hijacked a little over twenty-four hours ago. There are over two hundred men, women, and children, being held hostage by the world's most feared terrorist, Ockbar Shalam. Shalam has demanded that his brother, Ahmed Shalam, be released into his custody. Ahmed is being held in a federal prison here in the United States and is scheduled to be executed next month. This story has some interesting twists to it, but right now we have to take a station break. When we return, we will meet the man who engineered the capture of Ahmed Shalam."

Patton, Bobby, and Tommy were focused on the broadcast. Tommy had arrived much earlier but had been busy with the media. Everyone was preoccupied with his own thoughts. Bobby was still concerned with the President's safety. There were too many people around he did not know or trust. Tommy's thoughts were focused on Dooley. He was interested to hear what fires Dooley would light that he would have to extinguish. The president was thinking about his wife. There was not much he could do for Katherine at this point, but would Katie understand? Would this be something that drove a wedge between them?

When the broadcast resumed, the execution tape was being shown in its entirety. Tommy looked over at the president. He appeared to be fine, but Tommy wondered what was going on inside his head.

"That was the execution tape from the terrorist leader," Mason said when the tape ended. "As you heard on the tape, Ockbar Shalam referred to the President's mother. This maniac is threatening to kill the president's mother if his demands are not met. The president's mother died years ago in an automobile accident. His father died serving his country. Katherine Morrison, the president's mother-in-law, was on Flight 454. The entire staff, at Channel 8 want to apologize right now, if we put Ms. Morrison in more danger than she is already in. As most of you know, Channel 8 first aired this story last night, before we had the execution tape in our possession. At that time, we had identified Ms. Morrison as the President's mother-in-law. We would not have done so had we known the terrorists thought she was his mother. Since this tape was made over twelve hours ago, and since this story has received such wide coverage, we are sure that they now realize exactly who Katherine Morrison is. We are very concerned with Ms. Morrison's safety and the well-being of the President's wife and entire family. We will lift them up in prayer. We have a special guest with us to help us understand how someone like Ockbar Shalam thinks, and the best way to end this situation. I want to introduce Senator Stewart Dooley, who orchestrated the successful capture of Ahmed Shalam. Thank you for joining us, Senator. I was not sure you would accept my invitation after our last meeting."

"My pleasure Ms. Mason," said Dooley. "Our last meeting was on election night, and I wasn't in the best of moods."

"Senator, before we get into the specifics about the hijacking, I want to talk about your relationship with the president. Seeing that the two of you have worked together before and were so successful, I would think you would be one of the first people called in to consult with him on a situation like this. I hear there is bad blood between you and President Patton. Is this because of the personal attacks you made against him during the presidential campaign?"

"No, it doesn't have anything to do with the campaign. For some reason, President Patton has always resented me. He has always been jealous of my success. I think the only reason he ran for President was to compete against me. When I was his commanding officer, he would always question my orders. I think he wanted to be me; he likes being in charge."

"Well, Senator, as the President, he is in charge. Have you offered him your services? How do you think he will respond to Ockbar Shalam?"

"Yes, I have offered my help, but he has refused it, which was his first mistake. This should have all been over with by now. The President should have handled this like the Osama bin Laden and Ahmed Shalam situations. My sources have informed me that the President knows exactly where the hostages are being held. A team of our Special Forces could have retrieved that plane an hour after it set down. It's too late for that now. He has lost the element of surprise."

"Senator, you sound as if all is lost. Are you confident of the safe return of the hostages? After all, President Patton did serve under your command."

"That he did, but I guess he is not as good a strategist as I thought. All is not lost, but the man has let too many opportunities slip away. He has made too many mistakes, and I doubt if he can recover."

"How do you think he will respond to Ockbar Shalam's challenge?"

"I can't tell you what his words will be, but I don't think he will measure up to our last two or three presidents in similar situations. I think he will appear weak and unsure. I think Ockbar Shalam will laugh at the man running our country. Pardon me for being so blunt, Ms. Mason, but I do not think Dale Patton is the man for the job. I believe all of the hostages will be killed, if they're not dead already."

"Do you have anything good to say about the President?"

"Give me a minute; I'm sure I can think of something."

"Is it too late for you and the President to work together on this?"

"The way the President has treated me, I have no desire to help him. I do, however, have a desire to return our citizens to their families. If the President were to ask for my assistance, I would help in any way I could, but the man is so damn arrogant, I doubt he will ask. Mark my words, Ms. Mason, before this is over, the fine people of this country will be disappointed with the man they elected to office."

"Hold that thought Senator. Right now, we have to take a break."

"Well," said Tommy, "it looks as if Senator Dooley is putting in a plug for General Dooley."

"Not to mention his I-should-have-been-president reference," said Bobby.

"Well, gentlemen, we didn't expect the man to sing my praises. Dooley is just being Dooley. He has a battleground mentality, in which there is no compromise. Someone has to win, and someone has to lose. To him, this is war, and everything goes. Right now, we are his enemy, and the terrorists are the weapons he is using against us. Besides, the more he takes credit for Ahmed's capture, the better fitting the noose becomes."

"You should expose what part Dooley actually played back then in your response to Ockbar," said Bobby.

"That would be vindictive Bobby, timely, but vindictive."

"I think it's a great idea," said Tommy. "That will change the focus from you trying to get the hostages out of this predicament to Dooley being the reason they are in it in the first place."

"That is something to think about. This is not the time though. I am sure the good Senator will give us plenty of opportunities to hang him. Quiet, the show is back on."

"Welcome back to Channel 8's coverage of the hijacking of AWA Flight 454. As of this moment, there are two confirmed deaths; one of the Secret Service agents assigned to the president's mother-in-law and the woman in the video who was so brutally murdered. We have been talking with Senator Stewart Dooley, a retired Marine Corps general. Senator, you mentioned something about the American people eventually becoming disappointed with President Patton. Give us a little more insight into why you feel this way."

"Well, Ms. Mason, it's no secret that Dale Patton is a living, breathing, walking mirage. He is not what he appears to be. Sure, he makes good speeches and talks tough, but when the going gets tough, he will fold like a cheap tent."

"How can you expect us to believe that? The man is a war hero and has a trunk full of medals to prove it. I think you are still upset because you lost to him in the election."

"I am sorry if the truth hurts, but you know I am not one to bite my tongue. As far as those medals are concerned, he can thank me for every one of them. If I wasn't constantly kicking his butt to keep him straight, he would have probably gone AWOL. The man used to be a decent soldier, but over the years, he has gotten soft. I just hope he has a lot of good people around him. If not, this country is in for some tough times under his administration."

"Thank you, Senator, for your comments. Ladies and gentlemen, our time is almost up. We will keep you informed on the hijacking situation throughout its entirety. In about thirty- minutes, the president will respond to the demands of Ockbar Shalam, and Channel 8 will carry it live. Also keep in mind what Senator Dooley has shared with us and see if it has any merit. I am Michelle Mason; join me right here after the president's response."

Immediately after the broadcast, Patton, Bobby, and the other advisors all met back in the same conference room in which they had viewed the execution. Tommy was the only new addition to the room. Patton began by addressing General Phillips.

"How are things shaping up General? Are we in position to take control of Iraqi airspace? Do we have U.N. approval?"

"No to both questions, Mr. President. Of the six countries that border Iraq, only Saudi Arabia and Kuwait have agreed to help us, and that was begrudgingly. It's almost as if they are banding together against us. Our planes are in route, but right now they will have to approach from Saudi Arabia. That is not terribly bad, since AWA Flight 454 is closer to that border. The U.N. will not give us approval just yet. They say that they do not have enough information on the matter and that we are moving too soon. They want proof Iraq is supporting the terrorists. The good news is that England and Germany are supplying us with air support, along with the carriers that go with them. It appears you have some very influential friends in England and

Germany. Mr. President, Iraq does not have a strong military, especially compared to that of the United States. Their Air Force consists of a few outdated fighters, a few helicopters and those big C-130s for transporting troops, supplies, and equipment. None of those bordering countries are a threat to our air superiority. Iran could cause a few more problems but not enough to lose sleep over, especially if we gain position first."

"Keep our planes on course. Tell them to go through Saudi Arabia's and Kuwait's airspace for now. However, give them the green light to fly over the other countries if they need to do so. Blame it on bad communication and inappropriate translation when the other countries contact us about it. We may have to go in without U.N. approval. I think they will come around once we get proof of Iraq's involvement. There will likely be no U.N. sanctions with England and Germany alongside of us. How are we positioned?"

"We have carrier fleets in both the Persian Gulf and the Mediterranean Sea."

"Why the Mediterranean?" asked Patton.

"It allows us to come from the northern and southern ends of the country and sweep everything toward Baghdad."

"Excellent; what else?"

"Once we secure airspace superiority, all military and commercial airstrips will be monitored. Upon your command, no planes or helicopters will be allowed to take off in Iraq. Our concern will be to watch our backs for possible allies coming in behind us. Per your command, our ground troops will form a perimeter five miles south of the location of AWA Flight 454 and five miles north of Baghdad. Besides the M2-A2 Bradley Fighting Vehicles, the ground troops will have continuous air support from A-10 combat planes and AH-64 Apache helicopters. The Apaches are under orders to take out all stationary or mobile missile launchers they come across. No one will be able to pass through those perimeters unless we allow it. Flight 454's location is well over 500 miles east of Iran and we doubt that anyone is heading in that direction. West of it is almost as many miles of countryside to cover, and we will be monitoring it."

"Good work. Once I start to broadcast, take control of the skies and set up the perimeters. You are approved to take any military action you have to in order to accomplish those goals. What about the evacuation of American citizens?"

"About 75 percent of them are out of harm's way as we speak," said Clermont. "The others are on the move but not quite out of harm's way. We just pray they will still be allowed to leave once you respond to Ockbar Shalam."

"What is the status on the Senate approvals, and the possibility of congress declaring this an act of war?"

"It doesn't look too promising, Mr. President," said Clermont. "The Senate will not give approval on such short notice; they have to convene and of course interrogate the people you want to place in various positions. They will, however, agree to temporary appointments until this mess has been cleaned up or they can go through the proper protocol for approving presidential appointees, whichever comes first. After an unofficial vote, congress will not declare this an act of war. They think you are moving too fast, and a few have murmured words such as 'unlawful' and 'impeachment.'"

"Those words don't bother me. I may go down in history as the President who served the shortest term ever, but Iraq will think twice before ever supporting terrorist acts against the United States again."

"Mr. President, it's time to head down to the set," said Bobby.

"I'm ready, good work guys."

Keith Turner and Marty Hickman opened the double doors as President Patton followed Bobby out of the room. The two guards outside of the door took a position on each side of the president. Keith and Marty followed behind him. They had walked about fifty feet when five additional agents joined in. Two agents walked along each side of Bobby. Two others took place on each side of the President, behind the two that were already there. The last agent fell in line with Keith and Marty. The entourage walked about a hundred feet down one corridor, turned left, and walked another fifty feet before reaching their destination. Armed military security personnel were stationed along the entire route.

President Patton, Bobby, and all of the agents but two entered the room. The two remaining agents closed the door behind the entourage and stood guard on the outside. They entered a small waiting area. There was a twenty-foot passageway into a much larger area. The President calmly sat down in the only chair that was in the waiting area. It was placed there specifically for him. It would be another ten minutes before he would go in front of the cameras.

The familiar sound of WADC, Channel 8 news was starting to broadcast live.

"Good evening, ladies and gentlemen, I am Sam Garrett, the Channel 8 Station Manager. In just a few moments, we will broadcast live President Patton's response to Ockbar Shalam, the terrorist responsible for hijacking AWA Flight 454. Late last night, we showed you a videotape that had been sent directly to us via our website. We will show you that video again in its entirety. However, I must warn you of the graphic violence depicted on this tape. Parental discretion is advised. Let's take a look."

Once again, the little old lady was shown being killed. She crumpled to the ground as two rounds were pumped into her lifeless body. Fear and hopelessness overwhelmed the other hostages as they observed the slaying through the windows of the aircraft.

Garrett reappeared on camera. He was standing in front of a raised platform, which included a podium loaded with microphones and containing the Presidential Seal.

"That is truly a disturbing piece of film," said Garrett. "As you heard at the end of the tape, this psychopath threatened to kill more people if the President did not respond in person. We will have his response when we return from this commercial break."

During the commercial President Patton, Bobby, Marty and Keith all entered the viewing area. The rest of the security detail stayed in the waiting area and the passageway between the two rooms. They entered from behind a white curtain that stretched from the ceiling to the floor, and ran the length of the room. On the other side of the curtain were the raised platform and the television crew. Three television cameras were ready to cover the live broadcast. Camera one was thirty feet away, directly in front of the podium. Cameras two and three were also thirty feet away and were placed at forty-five-degree angles from the podium. They were to the left and right of the president.

The president waited behind the curtain until he was introduced. Bobby, Marty and Keith entered the room first. They walked the length of the room and checked out everything. Other than the camera and production crew, no one but security personnel was allowed in the room.

"Does everything check out over there?" asked Keith, as he spoke through the mouthpiece from his headset.

"Everything looks good," Marty replied.

Keith reached down to his control box and clicked a button. He switched channels so that he could talk to Bobby. The rest of the Secret Service was on a separate channel from Bobby and his men. In the meantime, Garret was coming back to introduce the President.

"Chief, one of the cameramen is unknown. The man on camera one is not the same person who was cleared earlier this morning. I recognize the operators on cameras two and three. I have no idea who is on camera one."

"A split-second later, three of Bobby's men entered the room. One agent stayed with the president, while the other two went to opposite sides of the room and stationed themselves directly behind cameras two and three. Bobby walked down the left-hand side of the room and crossed the floor to cover camera one. He stood to the right of the cameraman as Keith kept an eye on Marty, who was in the back of the room behind camera one.

"Ladies and gentlemen, the President of the United States," Garrett said gesturing toward the curtains.

President Patton walked through an opening in the middle of the curtain. He climbed the steps of the platform and walked to the podium. The agent stood to his right, just out of the picture.

The president appeared extremely relaxed, although he knew something was wrong. He had been around Bobby long enough to know his protocol. He looked rested and alert. There was no prepared statement to read from and no teleprompter, which caught the attention of the station manager. The President stood tall, placed his hands on each side of the podium, and looked directly into camera one.

"Ladies and gentlemen, I address you live for the first time as your President. I would have preferred to do so with a more motivating message, but that was not to be."

Bobby watched every move of the operator on camera one. He noticed a small, metal box attachment to the side of the camera. If you did not know better, you would have thought that it was an original part. The end of the box that faced the operator was open, just big enough for a man's hand. There was no such attachment on the other cameras. Bobby positioned himself for a better look. The cameraman moved his right hand toward the opening of the box.

Without warning, Bobby yanked the cameraman's right arm out of the box and twisted it back away from the camera. Simultaneously, he covered the operator's mouth with his left hand. The man had grabbed a pistol, which discharged. A spitting sound was followed by a muffled thump, followed by a loud cracking noise and a groan. A silencer on the barrel of the pistol caused the spitting sound, and the muffled thump was the discharged round that lodged into the ceiling. Bobby had broken the man's arm at the elbow, which caused him to let out a muffled scream of pain.

When Bobby released the arm, it dangled like a wet noodle. Unable to use his hand, the pistol fell to the floor. Bobby quickly struck the would-be assassin in his temple, rendering him unconscious. The agent behind camera three came over and took charge of camera one. Two agents entered the room and carried the assassin out. They were careful to stay out of the live broadcast at all times. Bobby stayed near camera one. The president witnessed the whole thing but did not miss a beat.

"AWA Flight 454 was hijacked and has landed in Iraq," he said. "There are over two hundred people on board, and the majority of them are American citizens. Ockbar Shalam, a well-known terrorist, wanted in over twenty countries, is taking credit for this cowardly deed. Shalam's brother is in a federal prison and will be executed in twenty-eight days. Shalam has threatened to kill all the hostages if his brother is not released. He also insisted that I appear live on this telecast to give my reply or more hostages would die."

"My official reply to him is that the United States of America does not negotiate with terrorist. We do not politely ask for something to be returned after it has been taken from us by force. We demand that it be returned or the terrorists will face severe consequences. Ockbar Shalam is the face behind this deed, but we have proof that Iraq is the fuel driving the engine. Therefore, I am holding that country responsible. We know that Ockbar and his minions are holed up in an abandoned military base south of Baghdad, near Karbala. We could have taken him out minutes after he landed, but Ockbar is merely the joker, and I am after the ace of spades."

"Iraq, you have seventy-two hours to return AWA Flight 454 and its passengers. You will pay a heavy price for every person who has been harmed or killed. As I speak, we are taking control of the airspace over your country. No military or civilian aircraft will be allowed to leave the ground. Any resistance will be met with the full force of the United States military. If AWA Flight 454 and its passengers are not released within seventy-two hours, Iraq will be turned into a parking lot. Correction," said the President as he looked at his watch, "you only have seventy-one hours and fifty-two minutes. You have been warned."

The President turned and left the podium. Bobby and the agent on the platform led him out of the room. The other agents circled the President, keeping him surrounded on all sides.

CHAPTER TWELVE

The skies of Iraq started to fill with English, and German fighter planes. The US Air Force ordered commercial planes to land at the nearest airstrip immediately. Iraqi military bases and large airports were heavily monitored. Large cargo planes dropped off troops and equipment south of the hostage site and north of Baghdad. The Persian Gulf supported aircraft carriers and destroyers.

A few fighter planes dropped bombs around the hostage site. They were instructed not to hit any buildings and to leave the main airstrip intact. The President was merely wanted to let Ockbar Shalam know that he was aware of his location. The city of Baghdad was not touched, but a couple of well-placed missiles convinced the Iraqi military to stay put.

"The United States of America does not negotiate with terrorists."

Ockbar watched the President on his television set. He did not utter a word as he studied Patton's eyes. He examined the President's face and mannerisms. He noticed that the President was not reading from a script. Ockbar was somewhat impressed by the confidence in the president's voice and his demeanor. He even liked the way President Patton ended his message and left. However, he did not like the way Patton addressed Iraq and him. The President was giving Iraq the credit that he deserved.

"This President means business," he said, as a devious smile spread across his face.

"I don't think this man appreciates your talents," said Rahman.

"He will appreciate me more after my next production. I think I will call it, 'The Funny Expressions People Make When Tortured,'" Ockbar said, as he, Rahman, and two other terrorists burst into hysterical laughter. "Bring me the first mother when the bombing stops."

He held his stomach in an effort to keep himself from laughing so hard. The two terrorists stumbled out of the room in laughter. Ockbar and Rahman tried to focus on the media's analysis of the president's response. They had just managed to calm down when Ockbar's cell phone rang.

"What the hell is it?" Ockbar snapped, still holding his stomach. "No, I did not know it was you. They cannot have anything. We have been very careful. The American president is bluffing. Listen to me. I heard what he said but he cannot do that, because it would start a war. We received a couple of shells also, but it was just a scare tactic. He may know where we are but he cannot prove Iraqi support. Get your allies to get them to back off." Ockbar ended the call.

"It sounds as if someone is not too happy," said Rahman.

"Something is not right. I have never heard the Prime Minister so desperate. The American President has put fear in his heart. That is hard to believe. We have been in tough situations before."

"He is getting too old for this kind of work. Maybe it is time for new leadership."

"That is not a bad thought Rahman, but now is not the time. He was saying something about Iraq being at the mercy of the Americans, and that we are sitting ducks."

"Why would he say that?"

"He said the Americans have control of the sky. We have no effective air attack against them, and our anti-aircraft weapons are too few to make a difference. That is when I mentioned Iraq's allies."

The two terrorists returned with Katherine. She yanked her left arm away from the grasp of one of them when they entered the room, and directed a comment at Ockbar.

"Those bombs hit pretty close. My son knows exactly where we are. I am sure that you realize he doesn't negotiate with people like you."

Ockbar left his chair and walked over to Katherine. He cocked his right hand back from behind his left ear and delivered a ferocious backhand. Katherine's head bounced and bobbed like a dashboard dog. She fell to her hands and knees. For a few moments, the right side of her face was numb. She could not feel the blood oozing from the cut on her cheek. The right side of her face darkened from her cheek to her chin. The burning sensation she began to experience was the feeling returning to her face. She struggled to look up at Ockbar. The force of the blow had wrenched her neck. As much as she hurt, she did not shed a single tear.

"That is for lying about who you are. You will pay for trying to make a fool of me. I will find out if you are as tough as you pretend. I will also give your son-in-law some convincing reasons why he should do everything in his power to keep me happy. Get three others from the plane and take the four of them to my workshop. Tell Abdul to grab his camera; we have another production to shoot."

Ockbar turned and walked back over to Rahman.

"As I was about to say, The prime minister thinks we slipped up somewhere. He is convinced the Americans actually have proof that the Iraqi government is financing this little venture. I think he is scared this president will carry out his threat of annihilation."

"You believe he is bluffing?"

"I believe he has bitten off more than he can chew. There is no way the UN, or even his own country, will allow him to kill innocent men and women."

"What if he already has their approval?"

"Don't tell me you are getting scared as well?"

"No man scares me; you should know that. I just wonder if you have underestimated him."

"I think it is just the opposite. The American President underestimates me. Just because he drops a few bombs close by, he thinks I will panic and run. Apparently this man does not know me. He does not know what I am capable of. He will learn."

Katherine was taken to the large empty room down the hall. One terrorist opened the metal door, and the other pushed her inside. She fell to her hands and knees as the door was closed and padlocked. There were two dimly lit bulbs hanging from the ceiling on a chain. This was the only source of light. There was just enough light to allow your imagination to get the best of you.

Cold, weak, and hungry, Katherine crawled across the concrete floor and sat in the farthest corner from the door. With her back against the wall, she brought her knees to her chin and wrapped her arms around her legs. She gently leaned her head back against the wall to relieve the pressure from her sore neck. Her eyes began to adjust to the dark, damp room, and she began to realize why Ockbar referred to this place as his workshop.

She began to tremble. The things she saw frightened her. The positive energy she tried to maintain vanished with one glance around the room. Shackles hung from each wall, except the one containing the door. All four walls were filled with bullet holes. She was sure they were bullet holes, because she saw a few shell casings scattered over the floor. Dark stains decorated the walls and the floor like a floral pattern. She closed her eyes. Her mind was conjuring up every hideous torture known to man, attempting to determine the history of those terrible stains.

Fear had taken root again and she shook uncontrollably. "No," she whispered to herself softly. "You cannot break me. You will not break me."

She took a few deep breaths, and began reciting The Lord's Prayer, which calmed her. Tired and sore, she decided to try and get some rest. Sleep would not be possible, although she had stopped shaking. She lay down in the corner and curled up in the fetal position. A sharp pain in her side kept her from getting comfortable. For a moment, she thought she had a bruised rib, but her throbbing cheek reminded her that she was struck in the face. She was lying on something. Reaching under her side to pull out what she thought would be a shell casing, Katherine was unnerved with what she saw. Between the index finger and thumb of her left hand was the largest molar she had ever seen. She quickly tossed the tooth aside, wiped her hand on her slacks, and sat upright. Tears rolled down her cheeks. She buried her head in her hands and quietly wept.

A voice came through the door from the hallway:

"Move along! Stop dragging your feet! You people act as if you have never faced death before."

Katherine's head popped up. She heard metal against metal. She wiped the last tear from her face just as the door swung open. The terrorists had shoved two men and a woman inside and locked the door behind them. They had not noticed Katherine sitting in the dark corner across the room, but she watched every move they made. A white man, a black man, and a white woman stood in the center of the room. They surveyed their cell, looking directly in Katherine's direction, but still not seeing her. Their eyes were still adjusting to the dimly lit, shadowy room, plus Katherine was wearing a black pant suit, which made her harder to see in the dark. All three seemed to be in their thirties.

The black man, whose name was Mike, walked back over to the door. He started checking the bars and the concrete around it to see if anything was loose. He looked up at the ceiling to see if there was any chance of an escape.

"It's no use Mike, said Tony, the white man. "We're dead and you know it."

"Just my luck," Mike said. "I end up spending the last few moments of my life with an asshole who keeps reminding me that I am about to die. Let me give the two of you a little advice. Terrorists thrive on fear, so when the time comes, die with a little dignity."

"Oh, I see," Tony said. "I should be macho like you and go down fighting," said Tony.

"You're damn straight. Die like a man."

"Shut up!" shouted the woman whose name was Susan. "Aren't things bad enough? What difference does it make how we die? We will be just as dead, whether we're smiling or crying."

She slumped to her knees in tears. Tony kneeled down and put his arms around her. His efforts to comfort her were therapeutic, but he looked as if he needed comforting himself. He sat down on the hard, concrete floor and curled one leg under the other in the lotus position. Susan sat down next to him, and Tony put his arm around her. He brushed her hair from her face with his free hand.

"You two can feel sorry for yourself some other time," Mike said. You need to come over here and help me with these bars. A couple of them are loose. We just can't give up without trying. This ain't much but it's all we got."

"Mike is right," Katherine said breaking her silence. "You should listen to him."

Mike stopped pulling on the bars and turned toward the direction of the voice. Susan and Tony sat up straight and focused on the dark corner were the voice had come from. Squinting to get a good look, they could only see the shadowy outline of someone. Tony stood up, pulling Susan up with him. Slowly they backed away until they almost bumped into Mike.

"Damn, I hope I never have to go into battle with you. Use your head. First, that's the voice of a woman, and second, she seems to be in the same predicament as the rest of us. Who are you? Show yourself."

"My name is Katherine. You will be able to see me a little better in a few moments, once your eyes adjust to the darkness."

"I know who you are," said Mike. "Now I recognize your voice. You're the one who helped that old guy when his wife was killed. I thought they had already killed you."

"Haven't you heard?" said Tony. "She's related to the new President. She is their prize possession, their bargaining piece. They will not kill her, at least not until they get what they want. By the way, what do they want?"

"On the plane," Katherine said, "Ockbar Shalam, the leader, told my bodyguard that the only reason he was letting him live was to tell the president to release his brother, who is being held in a federal prison in the states. He is accused of being the mastermind of numerous bombings and murders. I think the bastard just wants to humiliate the president and is using his brother as an excuse. If it wasn't his brother, it would be something else."

"Well, what's the holdup," asked Tony. "Why doesn't the president give the creep his brother so we can go home? Surely more than two hundred people are worth the life of one terrorist!"

"It's not quite that simple, Tony," said Mike. "The terrorists plan to kill all of us anyway. You can't trust them. That's why law enforcement doesn't like to negotiate."

"Every president is tested by terrorists," Katherine said. "I bet President Patton didn't expect his test to come so soon. Not to mention, Ockbar's brother was actually captured by the current president, who had strong messages about anti-terrorism in his campaign speeches."

"To make a long story short, you're saying we are going to die no matter what?"

"That's a good possibility, Tony. That's why you should be helping Mike with those bars."

"This is not right!" cried Susan. "This was just a vacation. A simple vacation! I saved and planned for three years for this? This cannot be happening. I am just thirty-one years old. Why am I about to die in a cold, dark cell in the middle of nowhere? It's a bad dream, that's what it is. I'll just lie down and go back to sleep. When I wake up, everything will be back to normal. My little fluffy dog will lick my face and wake me up like he always does. This is just a bad dream; I'm not going to die."

Trembling, Susan sat back down on the floor. Tony sat down beside her. She laid her head on his lap. Susan mumbled to herself, nervously rocking back and forth. Tony put his arm around her and tried to reassure her everything would be okay. It took a while, but eventually, she stopped trembling.

CHAPTER THIRTEEN

"Good work, Bobby. Take me to him!" said Patton with anger in his voice.

"Yes, Mr. President," answered Bobby. "He is Special Agent Dennis Kelpler with the CIA. He served under Dooley while in the Marines. Now he works for Pitts. He has a wife, three kids, and twenty-eight years of government service under his belt. His last two bosses just happen to be your two biggest fans."

Patton, Bobby, and the rest of the armed entourage exited the live telecast and walked one hundred feet down the corridor. They went down one flight of stairs, turned left and walked another fifty feet. Two armed soldiers stood guard at a doorway, and two additional soldiers kept watch over the assassin. Keith Turner was the only one allowed to enter the room with Bobby and the president. The two soldiers in the room were ordered to wait outside.

The room was not very big. A small, square metal table was bolted to the floor in the middle of the room. The prisoner sat in a folding chair. These were the only items in the room. Dennis Kelpler's seat was on the opposite side of the table, facing the door. His left wrist was handcuffed to a ring-shaped steel bar, which was imbedded in the table. The steel was an inch in diameter and solid. The entire ring was eighteen inches in diameter, with half of it hanging from beneath the table and the other half protruding from the top. Kelpler was handcuffed over the top of the table. The table included two other similar rings on both sides adjacent to the prisoner. Kelpler's right arm swung freely from the elbow. His upper arm, above his elbow, looked perfectly normal, but the palm of his hand faced outward away from his body. He had been revived and was in obvious pain. As soon as the door closed behind the two soldiers, Patton approached the prisoner.

"Who hired you to kill me?"

Kelpler did not speak. His dark brown hair was soaked from sweat that was running down his face. He bent over and rested his forehead on the table. His breathing was heavy and labored.

"I'm listening," continued Patton. "Give me the name and testify against this man, and your family will not lose your pension. It would be a shame to throw twenty-eight years of service down the drain with nothing to show for it."

"My kids are grown; they can take care of themselves," Kelpler said, raising his head.

"What about your wife?"

"You mean the bitch that was screwing a twenty-three year old army corporal? May she rest in hell."

"I'm not after you, Kelpler. I want the mastermind behind this little scheme. Help me bring him down, and you will be out in twelve years with good behavior."

Kelpler was silent once more. He laid his head back down on the table. His jaws moved as if he was about to speak, but nothing came out. Keith rushed to the prisoner's side and grabbed him under the neck with his left hand, while trying to pry his mouth open with his right. He was too late. Kelpler's head slumped to one side.

"What in the hell is going on?" asked Patton.

"Cyanide tablet," answered Bobby. "Keith tried to keep him from biting into it, but he didn't get to him in time."

"Chief, come and take a look at this," said Keith.

As Bobby moved in closer, Keith lifted a necklace that had been hidden beneath Kelpler's shirt. At the end of the chain was a coin, an Indian-head nickel. Bobby ripped the chain from the dead man's neck.

"You know, this is the only thing I really liked about Dooley," Bobby said as he handed the necklace to Patton. "He liked the African American platoons of the Civil War. He admired the Buffalo Soldiers."

"Dooley's calling card," said Patton as he examined the coin. This is too easy. Dooley is not that stupid."

"Exactly what I was thinking," said Bobby.

"Maybe we are over-estimating the Senator," said Keith. "Or maybe this guy isn't as smart as Dooley thought he was. Personally, I think Dooley was in a hurry to get rid of you, sir, and used what was available at the time, and what was available is a little sloppy."

"Explain," ordered Patton.

"Sir, Marty Hickman is your snitch. Before I called the chief to report a different operator on camera one, I asked Marty if everything checked out. He gave me the okay, but he was with me when we first checked out the room and the camera operators. He had the opportunity to point out the replacement but he didn't. I refuse to believe he did not catch it. We all know that Marty served under Dooley. From my understanding, Marty idolized the guy."

"Good job, Keith," said Bobby, "but Dooley didn't assign Marty to the President, Pitts did."

"Why don't I just bring him in here and beat it out of him? We can find out right now who he's working for."

"No, that probably wouldn't do any good," said Patton. "He would deny everything and know that we were on to him. Besides, Dooley and Pitts could be working together. I want both of them. I don't want to leave any loose ends for one of them to come at me again in a few months. Here, Keith, put Dooley's calling card in Kelpler's pocket. Phones will start ringing when Marty finds out about that necklace, and that will be the beginning of the end."

Keith took the necklace as instructed and put it in the right hip pocket of the corpse. Bobby and Keith led the President out of the room. The two soldiers returned to their posts but stopped in their tracks when they saw the prisoner slumped over the table.

"Check his mouth," instructed Bobby. "He bit into a cyanide tablet. I think our questions were giving him a headache."

All of the agents of the entourage re-formed the security barrier around the president, except Marty. As they walked down the corridor, Patton, Bobby and Keith, noticed that Marty stayed behind.

"The rat has gone after the cheese," replied Bobby.

When Patton and his entourage returned upstairs, they were met by dozens of reporters. They were almost refusing to allow the president to pass. They were persistent in their attempt to question the president. Bobby was about to push his way through them when Patton stopped him.

"What can I do for the press," Patton asked nonchalantly, as if he didn't already know?

"Tell us about the assassination attempt," replied one of the reporters.

"There is really not much to tell at this time. The individual behind camera one, who shall remain nameless for now, was not the scheduled operator. Luckily, Bobby and his men stopped him before he could complete his assignment."

"Was he working alone?" asked a different reporter.

"Has he said why he tried to kill you?" asked another.

"The individual is dead. He bit down on a cyanide tablet that he had hidden in his mouth. He died before we could get any information from him. Therefore, we don't know if he was working alone or what his reasons were."

"Mr. President, is it true this man worked for the FBI?"

"No, actually he was with the CIA."

"Who are your suspects, sir, and why is the CIA trying to kill you."

"Let's not jump the gun. I said that he worked for the CIA. We have no idea if the department was behind this or not. That is all we know at this time. Excuse me, gentlemen, but I have hostages I am trying to rescue."

Bobby, Patton, and the rest of the entourage continued without resistance. The reporters scattered, each one trying to be the first to send in their story. Patton returned to his office, where Darrin and Tommy were waiting for him. Bobby went inside the office with Patton while Keith and another one of Bobby's men guarded the door from the outside. The other agents patrolled the halls and stairways.

"Anything else you want to tell us about the assassination attempt?" asked Tommy.

"There is not much more to say at this time," said Patton. "We're just waiting for the rat to take the bait."

"What bait? Is Dooley behind this?" asked Darrin.

"Probably," said Patton, "we found his calling card, an Indian-head nickel, on the guy. We put it back in his pocket, as if we hadn't seen it. Once discovered, we think it will create quite a buzz. We believe that Marty Hickman is the snitch; he remained behind when the rest of us left. We figure the rat has the cheese now, and we want to see who he shares it with. "

"At least we know who to watch what we say around. I am sure Bobby has your safety under control; it's your political life I am concerned about."

"Either way, I'll be fine. Iraq is behind the hijacking. All I have to do is prove it. Speaking of proof, have you found out anything?"

"No, but I am working on a lead. Three days is not very much time, you know. I hope you're braced for the fallout, because the media and everyone else will be trying to crucify you."

"My only concern is bringing the hostages home alive and sending a very strong message to whoever is behind all of this. If I am able to do that, it doesn't matter what anyone thinks. How is Katie holding up?"

"She is about as well as can be expected under the circumstances. She will not get any better once the media starts putting ideas in her head. They will try to pit the two of you against each other by trying to convince her that your threats against Iraq have made her mother's death inevitable."

"I don't make threats, terrorists make threats. That was a promise."

"Mr. President, we are not the ones you have to justify anything to," Darrin said. "I am just trying to prepare you for the media onslaught, which will no doubt be fueled by your friends in Congress. I think you should make it a point to watch the eleven o'clock news tonight. It should be very interesting. Come on, Tommy, we have work to do."

Darrin and Tommy left the room. Bobby watched his old friend pace the floor. He noticed a strange expression on Patton's face, one he had never seen before. It was not one of fear, anger, or frustration. The President was in a state of turmoil. The indecisiveness showed on his face. Bobby had never known Dale Patton to second-guess himself.

CHAPTER FOURTEEN

Katie had just watched her husband's live broadcast. She could not believe her ears. She knew Dale would not negotiate with the terrorists, but she did not expect him to act so quickly. Three days was a little quick to start a war. Three days was not enough time to bring her mother back alive, especially since her identity had been disclosed. Katie had been speaking at a center for abused women when the telecast aired. She wanted to do something to take her mind off of her mother and at the same time prove she was confident everything would turn out for the best. This had turned into a major mistake. The media inundated her before the telecast was over. Even with bodyguards, she and her assistant, Emily Langston, could not make it to her waiting limousine without being interrogated.

"Excuse me, Katie, what do you think of your husband's decision?" a reporter asked as he maneuvered his way into earshot?

"Will this hinder the safe return of your mother?" hollered another.

"What about your platform on family values?" asked yet another. "How are you holding up under this ordeal? Will you and the President stay together if your mother doesn't come back alive?"

"Did you know of his decision before he went on the air?"

"Do your mother and the President get along?"

"You realize the President has signed your mother's death warrant, don't you?"

The questions kept coming and coming and coming. Before Katie could attempt to answer a question, she was asked three more while cameras rolled, and bulbs flashed. She felt weak in the knees, as if she was about to pass out. She felt herself losing control. Emily helped her to the car. It was just a few feet away, though it seemed like miles. After she was finally locked safely inside, Katie drew strength from deep inside and gave one of the best performances of her life. As the limousine pulled off, Katie displayed a very convincing smile and winked at the reporters. Then the limousine sped away.

Before the limousine reached the Whitehouse, Katie felt her strength returning. She felt a little weak, but she was okay. She could not help but think of the comments the media had bombarded her with. Some of them hit too close to home. She was relieved that she had maintained her composure. She could just imagine her picture on the front page of the morning paper, sprawled out in the back of the limousine. What a field day the media would have had with that.

Upon entering the Whitehouse grounds, Katie was distraught at what she saw: Another flock of media vultures greeting the limousine. She would not go through this again. Extra security was called for from the car. Dozens of agents appeared and cleared a path for Katie and Emily. They managed to enter the Whitehouse without incident.

Once inside, the two women hurried off without saying a word to anyone. Upon reaching the elevator Katie pressed the up button. When the elevator finally arrived, the doors could not open and close fast enough for her.

"Is there anything I can …"

Before Emily could finish, the elevator doors had closed, and Katie was out of sight. When the doors reopened, Katie ran to her office and locked the door behind her. Moving very slowly, she walked over to her desk and sat down. She was confused. Her head was beginning to spin, and she could feel herself getting dizzy. Something in her peripheral vision caught her attention. Looking to her right, Katie noticed the message light on her phone was blinking profusely. After wrestling with this decision for about fifteen minutes, she decided to listen to her messages. She reached over and pressed the Play button and soon realized she had made the wrong decision.

Elected official after elected official had called to give their condolences. The wives of elected officials had called, doing the same thing. There were two dozen messages, which was more than she could take. Everyone was assuming her mother was already dead. She turned the messages off after listening to a few of them. Her anger made her forget about how bad she had felt just moments earlier. She needed answers, and her husband was the only one who could give them to her. Without hesitation, she picked up the phone and called him.

Patton was sitting alone, watching a live broadcast of the media critiquing his response to Ockbar Shalam, when Bobby entered the room. These specials had been on all day. It seemed as if every station had a celebrity, politician, psychologist, psychiatrist, human behavior specialist, or some kind of military expert on their show, giving their opinion of the president's response. Person after person, mostly elected Republican politicians, and a few Democrats, continued to berate the president and find fault in every decision he had made up to this point.

Bobby watched for a few moments before he realized what the President was doing. He was making a mental note of the ones who found fault in everything he had done thus far. Bobby smiled. Patton was back to his old self.

"Yes, Bobby, what can I do for you?"

"Katie is on line three, Mr. President. She sounds a bit pissed. From what I have heard, that is better than she has been."

"Thanks Bobby, I'll take it in here," said Patton as he found the remote and turned down the volume on the television. He then picked up the telephone receiver and punched line three on the base of the phone.

"Hello Katie."

Bobby left the room and gently closed the door behind him.

"I need some answers, Dale, and I need them now."

"What is it, dear?"

"Don't patronize me Dale. Do you really dislike Mother that much? I saw your response to this situation. How can you throw her life away like that, not to mention the hundreds of other people who are on that plane? I thought you liked my mother. I thought your squabbling was just your way of showing affection for one another."

"You have known me for a long time Katie. You know that I like your mother. Do you really think I would put her life at risk?"

"I didn't think so, but now I'm not so sure. Dale, you are about to start a war, for God's sake! Do you have proof that Iraq is behind the hijacking?"

"No, not yet."

"Not yet? What do you mean, not yet? You have just threatened another country with military force off of a gut feeling? That's insane, Dale. You have to back off for Mother's sake and for everyone else on that plane. No wonder the media and everybody else is blasting you. There's no method to your madness."

"Now we're getting to the heart of the matter. I see what's going on now."

"What are you talking about? What the hell do you see?"

"It looks as if the media has gotten to you. What did they tell you? That I had killed everyone aboard that plane? Did they tell you I wanted your mother out of the way and this was the perfect opportunity? I am surprised at you Katie. I thought you were smarter than that. I know this has been tough on you, but don't let the media manipulate you. You know as well as I do that terrorists like Ockbar Shalam never release hostages alive. You know the chances of your mother returning alive are a million to one. They are probably higher than that, since she is the pawn Ockbar is using to try and force my hand. Like I said, Katie, you have known me for a long time. You know I never act on anything this important unless it has been carefully thought out. Why would this be any different?"

"I think you're in too deep Dale and are too proud to admit you made a mistake. People's lives are on the line. You have to try and negotiate with these people."

"Listen to yourself, Katie. Can you hear yourself? You're asking me to negotiate with people who don't have a conscience. You know

I won't do that. You have known that for over thirty years. At this point, it would do more harm than good. I realize how hard this is on you, but more is at stake than your mother's life. More than two hundred other lives and the integrity of the strongest nation on earth are at stake also."

"I don't want to hear that military mumbo jumbo Dale. Just bring mother back alive. Bend a little, for once in your life."

"Don't you know terrorists thrive on the fear and weakness of others? Even if I thought I had made a mistake, which I haven't, admitting it would be the worst thing I could do at this point. That would seal Katherine's death for sure. If your mother survives this ordeal, it is because I am going about it in the only way that could possibly save her life. I knew I would catch a lot of flak about my decision, but never in my wildest dreams did I think you would turn against me too."

"I haven't turned against you, Dale. I just want Mother back alive. Is that too much to ask?"

Katie hung up the telephone before he could respond. She was angry and upset, but most of all she was concerned about her mother. Patton knew that as long as she held on to the anger, she would be okay. She could function through anger; she was actually sharper and more focused when she was angry. More than anything, he knew that the inability to help her mother was eating her up inside. As long as she was angry, she would not be feeling sorry for herself. He also knew that something or someone had gotten to her, because this was not like Katie.

He could feel himself getting angry. He was used to difficult and stressful situations at work, but he was not used to work problems affecting his personal life. He kept telling himself it was the nature of the job, but that did not make him feel better. Going after the terrorists responsible for this hijacking was a covert mission he would love to command. Grabbing Ockbar Shalam by the throat and squeezing the life out of him would make him feel a lot better.

Patton hung up the telephone, after holding it under his chin for a few moments, in deep thought. He picked up the remote and restored the volume on the television. Most of Congress had criticized him, speaking on live television to give their opinion of what he was doing wrong. Mostly, they were taking this opportunity to advance their own interest.

Saheed el-Ali, the Iraqi Prime Minister, was shown in a taped interview accusing the president of seeking personal gratification. He accused Patton of being a career soldier who could only find satisfaction through combat. Besides saying that President Patton was trying to control the oil trade of his country, he also accused him of trying to put an international feather in his cap at Iraq's expense.

The more he listened, the more determined Patton became. Except for a small circle of friends, everyone was attempting to hang him out to dry; everyone in Washington, that is. However, the public approved of his actions. In a national telephone poll conducted by Channel 8 News, the president had an 88 percent approval rating by the public. That kept him motivated.

As Patton listened to the last few minutes of the telecast, he noticed that the discussion turned toward the talk of impeachment. He knew it was coming. It was inevitable. At this time, the talk was more of a ploy to try to scare the president into changing his actions. Patton refused to reconsider, and he knew the impeachment process would eventually start. He also knew that if impeachment was imminent, it would not come in time to save Iraq, if the hostages were not released in the next sixty-four hours.

Patton was about to turn off the television. He wanted to get a few hours of sleep before the eleven o'clock news came on, but the next story caught his attention. Michelle Mason was doing a special piece about the President's popularity. The country loved how the new President was handling the hijacking situation. Mason was saying how most of the calls and emails were telling Washington to support the President or get out of his way. The people sided with the President and were making it known that they approved of how he was handling the hijacking situation. There were threats of nonsupport and a handful of small, peaceful demonstrations.

Patton liked what he heard. There had to be a way he could use this to his advantage. He turned off his television and lay down, with this being the last thing on his mind.

CHAPTER FIFTEEN

As Darrin had predicted, the media questioned every decision the president made. Patton sat and watched the eleven o'clock news with Bobby. Everyone gave their opinion on what the president did wrong and how the situation should have been handled. He was described as a trigger-happy soldier who knew nothing about politics or protocol. The first lady was painted as a high-society want-to-be on the verge of having a nervous breakdown. To make matters worse, Dooley had been interviewed for his opinion about the entire situation. Michele Mason gave Dooley more camera time than any of the other guest. He, of course, was the expert on terrorist activities and claimed to know Patton better than anyone. Patton listened intently as Dooley did his best to make the president look incompetent.

"The situation was handled all wrong," said Dooley, as he began to explain what should have been done. "First of all, we knew where the plane was every second, even when it landed. We could have had soldiers waiting on the plane when it set down. Those hostages could be home safe right now. There is no need to threaten an entire country. The President just over reacted. He will have us in another War with Iraq if he continues this line of action. I tell you, Michele, the man has cracked. I think impeachment procedures should start as soon as possible. Dale Patton is just another pretty face that tells the people what they want to hear. He has no substance."

"Senator, it sounds like you have a genuine dislike of the President."

WILLIAM I. BRAZLEY JR.

"We're not drinking buddies, if that is what you mean. I just want what is best for those poor hostages and what is best for the American people. Besides, some of your other guests voiced the same concerns."

"Yes, but none of them mentioned impeachment."

"None of your guest tonight spoke about impeachment, but it is being discussed. Few people are as blunt and straight to the point as I am. They are thinking it and talking about it behind closed doors. They just don't want to be the first to go on record on live television and say that Dale Patton should be impeached."

"Thank you, Senator, said Michelle Mason. "To recap what our distinguished guest had to say; most people in Washington are distancing themselves from the president. He is virtually on his own, except for a handful of followers. Congress has refused to back him, but the president has called a state of emergency, giving him the authority to exercise his powers as commander-in-chief of the armed forces. This in fact angered many congressional representatives. They feel that the President could be a loose cannon, determined to do things his way, no matter what."

"I believe Senator Dooley was correct when he stated that he was not the only one thinking of impeachment. I think it is on the mind of quite a few people here in Washington. I believe the powers-that-be think the wrong man was put into office. True, no one but Senator Dooley has said anything to that effect publicly, but there are a lot of closed-door conversations going on."

"According to our telephone poll, however, President Patton is still very popular with the American people. They like his hard stance on this issue. The President's actions are actually rallying the people around him. They are feeling safer as a country with a President who gets directly involved when they are in danger. A large percentage of the people surveyed, believe the United States should be more aggressive in responding to terrorist actions. They approve of the way the President is handling the situation. After all, President Patton did not mince words in his campaign speeches. He stated from the start that he believed in a strong military. He also stated that he believed the

United States was entirely too passive in similar situations. To be truthful, President Patton has not strayed from his campaign promises. Apparently, they were not just idle promises to get elected. He has been true to form. I think we did not realize the depth of his conviction, and did not expect to find out so soon in his administration."

"On the other side of the coin, Iraq is claiming total innocence. They claim to have nothing to do with AWA Flight 454. They insist Ockbar Shalam is acting independently, without support from the Iraqi government. Iraq is claiming that the United States is doing this out of greed. America doesn't like that Iraq controls the vast amount of the oil it produces, and is acting aggressively as a result, according to Prime Minister Saheed el-Ali. Now where have we heard that before? In fact, el-Ali goes so far as to claim that the United States staged the entire hijacking incident to justify attacking his country. The deputy prime minister emphasized that Iraq refuses to be bullied and will defend itself."

"The flip side of the story is that Iraq refused to help the United States in any way. Not only did they refuse to assist, they denied U.S. access across their borders and threatened military action against any attempt by the United States to search for the hostages. In essence, Iraq is providing an asylum for the people responsible: whom they say are acting independently. The president had two choices: try a long, drawn-out negotiation, which is usually non-productive, or take immediate action by holding someone responsible. I believe the President made the correct decision. This is Michele Mason, signing off for Channel 8 News."

"It looks as if Michelle Mason is in your corner," said Bobby. "That's a plus."

"That's about the only good news I have heard since this whole thing started," replied Patton. "Do you think things are starting to turn in our favor," he asked sarcastically.

"You'll feel better when we bust Dooley."

"That would make me feel good. I'm not so sure it would make me feel better. By the way, thank you for saving my life. I just realized I had not acknowledged your actions until now."

"I'm just doing my job, boss," said Bobby.

"And you do it very well, but it's too early to ask for a raise."

Patton and Bobby shared a good laugh.

"Tell me something, Bobby, do you think I'm doing the right thing, making the right decisions? I know I have not exactly followed protocol. People are dying because of my decisions, and now it's hitting home."

"Dale, when we were in combat, did you ever ask yourself if you were doing the wrong thing?"

"No, you don't have time to ask yourself anything when you're fighting."

"Exactly, and this is a fight. It's wrapped in politics, but it's a fight. If you're fortunate enough to make it through the fight, then you can sit down and ask yourself if you made the right decisions. In a fight, you go off of training and instinct. When you stop fighting and start thinking, you wind up on your back. I have gladly followed you in a lot of fights, and you know I just don't follow anybody. This is just another fight in a different arena, and you haven't done anything to make me regret it."

"Thanks Bobby. I guess I knew it deep down inside but I needed to hear it. I'm okay, just a little concerned about Katie."

"This is a shock to all of us, especially Katie, but she'll be fine. I know you're hurting a little inside but we're soldiers and trained not to let it show as much. Katie isn't a soldier, but she is a warrior and a fighter. She will lick her wounds for a while, but watch out, because she will come up swinging. I better leave so you can get some rest. No telling what tomorrow will bring."

"Do me a favor. Check to see if Tommy is still up. If so, ask him to come by here for a few minutes."

"I bet he's still up and would appreciate a good chat with you. Good move, boss, I'll send him in."

Bobby left the study, which connected to his bedroom, as Patton flipped through the channels. After the attempt on his life earlier, Patton knew Bobby would not leave his living quarters. Bobby called Tommy from the living room and informed him that Patton wanted to talk to him. Less than ten minutes later, Bobby was opening the door for Tommy.

Tommy looked a little bewildered. He wondered why the President wanted to see him at this hour, and in his private quarters. The door to the study was open, but Tommy knocked before entering.

"You wanted to see me Mr. President," he asked?"

"Yes, I do. Come on in Tommy, and since this is unofficial business, drop the 'Mr. President' routine."

That caught Tommy by surprise. He didn't know how to react. He wanted to smile, but he didn't want to be too relaxed and casual. Tommy and the President had been on a first name basis before he won the election, but he figured he should give Dale his due respect. He had called him Mr. President ever since, and until now had not been encouraged to do otherwise. He was excited and tingling all over, but he didn't want it to show."

"Thank you, sir, uh, I mean, I appreciate it, Dale. What can I do for you?"

"Have a seat Tommy and relax. I just want to talk to you for a bit."

Tommy did as he was instructed, but he had too much nervous energy to really relax. Outwardly, he looked fine but inside he felt awkward. He felt as if this was his coronation, so to speak. He was in the President's private quarters, sitting down and chatting with the most powerful man on earth. I'm being invited into his inner circle, Tommy thought. I'm finally one of the gang. Tommy had to stop thinking like that. He was starting to get nervous, and that would not be good.

"First," said Patton, "I want to compliment you on what a fantastic job you're doing. I know the first couple of days have been hell, but you have performed above my expectations, and I appreciate it."

"Thank you, sir," said Tommy. "It has been interesting, but I wouldn't miss a minute of it."

"I'm glad you feel that way. It would be a little more exciting for me if I didn't have a personal interest in the situation."

"I understand, sir."

"Tell me something Tommy; how do you have so many contacts, who are always in the right place?"

"I'll make a deal with you, sir. I'll tell you my secret if you tell me if you're really a lousy poker player or were just pulling my leg."

Patton laughed. "You're still thinking about that?"

"Yes sir, I am," said a smiling, more relaxed Tommy. "I think you guys were pulling my leg. I haven't been around you as long as some of the other guys, but you seem to do everything well; everything you have an interest in, that is. I have noticed that you don't seem too fond of protocol."

They both laughed.

"Touché," said Patton. "Well, Tommy I love playing poker, but some of it goes against some very deep, basic core beliefs. I am a lousy poker player because I never bluff. That's not restricted to poker; I never bluff in anything."

"You're serious aren't you?"

"Very serious," replied Patton.

"So, every threat you have made against Iraq, you plan to follow through?"

"I don't threaten, Tommy. To me, a threat is a disguised bluff, and I don't bluff…ever. I would not waste all of those military resources and risk the lives of brave men and women on a bluff. Those soldiers are around Iraq's borders and in their airspace for a reason, and I hope every last one of them is ready to carry out their mission if Iraq does not cooperate."

There were a few seconds of silence as Tommy's respect and admiration for his boss increased. He finally understood the directive the president gave him when he agreed to make him his press secretary. He also realized why people gravitated to him. There was no guessing about Patton. He was what he appeared to be. Either you liked him or you didn't, but there was no hypocrisy in him.

"Enough about me," said Patton. "Tell me how you get information before the media when you are thousands of miles away. You seem to have a heck of a network."

"That's one way to put it. It is a very extensive network that covers most of the world; and 99 percent of the time, I don't even know who is providing me information."

"How can that be?"

"Mr. President, I mean Dale, have you ever heard of a super spy who went by the name of Casper? Most everyone believes he was not real. The story goes that he was a fictional character created by the U.S. to intimidate some of our enemies and to keep them off balance. After all, who goes by the name of Casper?"

"Yes, I have heard of him. Supposedly, he was America's version of James Bond. He disappeared about twenty years ago and hasn't been heard from since. That's all I know about him."

"Do you believe he was real, or do you think he was a myth," asked Tommy?

"My experience has taught me that most myths originate from a thread of truth. I believe that there was no such person who could live up to all of the tall tales I have heard about this Casper, super spy. However, I do believe there was probably someone from whom the myth originated. I believe his success grew into gigantic proportions until he was larger than life, like an old fisherman telling about the big catch that got away. Why are you so interested in Casper? What does he have to do with your network?"

"I believe in Casper, because he was my father." Patton's eyes opened wide. Tommy had his full attention.

"You may be the third or fourth person in the whole world who has ever known that. Of course, my mom knew, and I think one other person that used to be a CIA operative knew.

He kept us a secret for obvious reasons. I can remember meeting my dad on only four or five occasions. The last time I saw him, I was eighteen years old and about to graduate from high school. He told me that he was going on an important mission and the odds were against him making it out alive. I had known since I was about ten that he was a spy. That was when he told me he was known in some circles as Casper because of the way he could disappear in plain sight."

"Are you telling me that Casper was real, that he was your father, and all of those super spy stories about him are true," asked Patton?

"Yes, I am saying he was real, he was my father, and depending on what you heard, those stories were mostly true. He was a master of disguise. He could speak six different languages, seven if you count English. He never counted English because he said it was a universal language that anyone could speak."

"Are you trying to tell me that your father is alive and giving you this information?"

"No, I am saying that through his many years of work, he had a lot of people in his debt.

A lot of them owed him their life. My father created this network for me. He told each person in his debt that he, or someone he appointed, would collect their debt to him by asking a favor. They were to grant whatever request was made of them. My father made sure the request was within their ability to grant, even money, if I should ask."

"So how does this work?

"My father set up a very organized and thorough data base, with hundreds, maybe even a thousand contacts. He lists their location, their trade, the languages they speak, why they were in debt to him and the things I could reasonably ask for and receive. He gave me a single phrase to say to remind the debtor of his or her promise. After that I merely had to ask for what I want, and make the arrangements to collect it if necessary."

Patton stared at Tommy in disbelief. He could not believe what he was hearing. This sounded like something off the silver screen, not something that happens in real life. He knew Tommy was telling the truth, but he still found it hard to believe.

"How often have you gone to this well," he asked?

"Not often," said Tommy, "only about a dozen times in my whole life, including the information that I received about the hijacking. My father advised me not to be selfish with my requests, and I haven't been. Though I must admit I did use it to get a certain job."

"Are you referring to the position as my campaign manager?"

"No, no, not at all," said Tommy. "I'm referring to a position I got years ago when I graduated from college. But I do think my dad may still be alive, hiding out somewhere, in retirement."

"Go on," said Patton, "tell me why you believe this."

"About twelve years ago, I received an anonymous package. In it was a disk with additional contact information on it. It had to come from my dad. It was in the same format and organized the same way as the information he gave me years before. Well, anyway, you asked, and that's the whole story. I would appreciate it if you keep this information between us. "

"It's still hard for me to believe all of this."

"As the President of the United States, you should know that you have this information at your disposal. I'd better be going. It's after midnight and you haven't gotten much sleep these last few days. Thank you, sir, for the chat."

"I should be the one thanking you. I promise to not take advantage of this information, but I will do everything I can to bring back as many hostages as I can."

"I understand," said Tommy. "Good night, sir."

"Good night Tommy. By the way, you were doing a great job even before you got me that information."

Tommy smiled, left the room, and gently closed the door. Bobby let him out and locked the door. The President sat still for a few minutes and thought about the conversation he just had. He tried to remember all of the things he had heard about Casper. He made a mental note to research this super spy and find out as much about him as he could. After all, if the President couldn't inquire about Casper, who could?

"I look pretty good on television," said Dooley as he watched the eleven o'clock news with a wide smile spread across his face. "Trashing Dale Patton comes easy for me. I would have done it at a bowling alley."

"I think the President knows more than he is letting on," said Marty. "I am sure he saw that buffalo nickel on Kelpler. He probably thinks you are behind the assassination attempt."

"Turn off the television," instructed Dooley, "and let me think for a minute."

Marty did as he was told. They were in a small luxurious room, reserved for visiting politicians and high-ranking officials. Dooley seemed somewhat relaxed. He sat on a plush couch with his feet propped up on a coffee table. Marty sat in a chair next to the couch.

"I shouldn't have anything to worry about, since I had nothing to do with that idiot's failure. However, knowing Dale as I do, he will try to pin it on me. The question is, why was my calling card found on his body? The answer is somebody is trying to frame me."

"Who else wants the President out of the way as much as you, and why would they frame you," asked Marty?

"There is only one person I can think of, and that is Nick."

"Are you referring to Bill Pitts, head of the CIA?"

"One and the same."

"Why would he frame you?"

"Because he knows everyone is aware of my hatred for Patton. I am the obvious choice. I would automatically be the number-one suspect, even without the buffalo head nickel. Nick knows the balance of power on the hill has changed dramatically since Dale has become president. I think he fears Dale will eventually maneuver him out of Washington. The bastard didn't have to set me up. I even offered to work with him."

"What are you going to do?"

"I'm not sure yet. I will be heading back to Washington soon, where I will give it a lot of thought. Don't worry, I'll keep in touch. I need to know everything Dale and Bobby are planning, so stay sharp. I might need your services before this is over."

"I'm on top of it boss, but how can you be so sure it was Bill?"

"Oh, it was him. I am sure of that. Find out whatever information you can. My plans may have just changed a bit. Since I didn't make president, maybe I can become the new Director of the CIA."

CHAPTER SIXTEEN

Patton was awakened by a knock at the door. He had fallen asleep on the couch before he had turned off the television. The light from the television, shining directly in his face, from an early morning news broadcast, had not disturbed him. Patton reached over to a lamp, on a nearby end table, and turned it on. The bright light hurt his eyes, and he covered them for a few moments with his hands. He looked at his watch and wondered why he was being disturbed at three o'clock in the morning. The knock came once more, with more authority this time.

"It's open," answered Patton.

Bryce Duncan and John Clermont walked in, followed by Bobby. Keith and Marty Hickman waited outside the room by the door. Three other agents had come with Marty and were waiting outside the door of the president's quarters. Security on the president had increased since the assassination attempt. At first glance, the president knew it was something concerning the hijacking.

"Spit it out," ordered Patton.

"Another tape from the terrorists was delivered about an hour ago," said Duncan.

"Where is it?" asked Patton.

Bryce removed the tape from his jacket and handed it to the president. Patton walked over to the television, powered up the Blu-ray player, and inserted the disc. He sat down on the couch as everyone else remained standing. Ockbar's toothy grin greeted the president as the video began.

"Hello, Mr. President," said Ockbar, "we meet once again. Apparently my first production was not convincing enough, so I have produced another short film for your enjoyment. I must admit it is getting more difficult to find volunteers for these roles. If you ask me, these roles are to die for."

Ockbar released a sarcastic laugh as the camera panned over to four individuals. As the picture came into focus, Patton could identify two men and two women. A white man, a black man and two white women were the unfortunate victims. They had been beaten so badly that they were hardly recognizable. They were on their knees, facing the camera, while a gunman could be seen behind them with a pistol in hand. There were other gunmen, with holstered weapons, surrounding the prisoners in the same formation as in the first tape.

First was Tony, who had one eye swollen shut and a split lip. His face was a rainbow of colors, bruised from a barrage of punches. Next to him was Susan, crying uncontrollably. It was not the loud cry of pain or anger but the soft muffled cry of hopelessness and despair. Her face was bruised and swollen as well. Blood trickled from her left ear; the result of a kick to the side of the head from a size eleven steel-toe boot. Next to Susan was Mike. He looked to have been beaten the worst, as if he may have offered some resistance. Both of his eyes were nothing but slits, and his nose was broken. Blood oozed from a gash on his head just over his right ear, and he was bent over in pain due to a few broken ribs. He was clearly having trouble breathing.

Patton winced in pain when he recognized the last woman. It was Katherine, peering straight into the camera with a look of defiance. Her face was swollen and disfigured as well. Her hair was all over her head and her left eye was almost swollen shut. She spat out a clump of blood. That brought a brief smile to Patton's face. She had winked her right eye at the camera right before she spat. That was her way of apologizing without actually saying it. She could always claim later that something was in her eye. This relieved Patton, for he knew his mother-in-law was not blaming him for this hostage situation.

The gunman walked up behind Tony and pointed the pistol at his head. After a moment's hesitation, he fired. The 32-caliber pistol was more than enough to do the job without blowing his head off. Tony fell face forward onto the hangar floor. The camera operator panned up toward the plane, showing the horror and fright on the faces of the other hostages, who were looking from the windows of the plane. One woman clutched at her mouth with both hands as her jaws inflated. She looked as if she was gagging, as if she was about to vomit. She quickly disappeared from the window. Another woman had both hands clasped in front of her face, with her head slightly bent, praying. The camera operator panned back down to the terrorist, who was still standing behind Tony's lifeless body with a smoking gun.

At the sound of the gunshot, the other three flinched in unison. Mike and Katherine hung their heads, but Susan became hysterical. She began to scream and cry, all the while begging for her life. The gunman took a step to his left and positioned himself behind her. He stood there for two full minutes as she begged and pleaded. When she paused to catch her breath, the gunman fired. The back of her hair flew up as she fell forward. She did not die instantly; she twitched and squirmed on the ground. The camera stayed focused on her until her body was finally at rest.

"Two down, two to go," said Ockbar as his voice was heard over the picture of Susan's limp body. "I hope you are starting to realize the consequences of your actions, Mr. President. If not, maybe these last two scenes will convince you."

The gunman stepped to his left once more. He was directly behind Mike, with his pistol aimed and ready. A shot rang out, and Mike fell forward. The gunman emptied three more rounds in Mike's lifeless body, and then spit on him. Katherine flinched with each shot. True to form, she remained calm as the gunman stepped to his left again and positioned himself behind her. His pistol was at his side and was not pointed at her yet, but she looked straight at Ockbar.

"I must congratulate you, Mr. President, on such a fiery mother-in-law," said Ockbar. "Of course, if she had not first told me she was your mother, she might not be in this predicament. Please explain to your wife how sorry you are for getting her mother killed. Oh, by the way, I expect to see you on the evening news again tonight, informing me that my brother has been released and is being delivered to me."

The gunman raised his pistol and placed it in the back of Katherine's head. She remained perfectly calm as he pressed the barrel against her head and shoved it forward a little. Katherine winked into the camera once more. At that precise moment, the picture went black. A split-second after that, a shot rang out. Ockbar's grinning face reappeared.

"Maybe you will be more cooperative this time. If not, I have plenty of film left," said Ockbar as the picture went black for good.

"Who all has seen this?" asked the President.

"Only the people in this room and Keith and Marty," answered Clermont.

"It was sent to Channel 8 again, but we intercepted it. Any type of communication sent from within a twenty-mile radius from that part of Iraq, into US territory, whether it is a television or radio signal, phone call, or email, will come directly to us. However, other countries can receive it and will probably be airing it in a matter of hours. We have a four-hour head start at best before the news starts airing it."

"We need to get to work, gentlemen," said Patton.

"That is not the only news, sir," said Clermont.

"What else is going on?"

"A few minutes before the tape arrived, Iran said our planes are compromising their airspace and warned us to leave. Russia says it is an ally of Iran, and they consider any threat to Iran as a threat against them. They have given us twenty-four hours to clear out."

"Or what?"

"Or they will return the firepower we dish out with equal or greater force."

"Equal?" "In some cases, that may be possible," said the president. "Greater force? Not in my lifetime."

Duncan and Clermont could do nothing but stare at the president. He was truly in a zone. He appeared extremely calm. He sounded more confident than he ever had, if that was possible.

"Let me take a wild guess," said Patton. "This came straight from the top brass of both countries, didn't it?"

"Yes sir, it did."

"I expected Iran to test us. The ayatollah is still living in the past, but we have something ready for him. I would have bet even money that Russia would have something to say, but never would I have bet they would align themselves with Iran. That Russian president is trying to use this incident as a way back into political prominence. He picked the wrong one, because he won't gain a reputation off us. Regardless of his reasons, the United States does not take threats from anyone, Russia included."

Bobby put his hand to his mouth and slightly turned his head. He was covering a large grin on his face.

"Well, gentlemen, it looks as if we have a new player in the game. Since Russia is vying for our attention, we will do just the opposite. Our military will prepare for her, but there will be no communication initiated by us on this matter. Richard, I want you and General Phillips to alert our world bases that Russia has joined the game, and to be prepared for aggressive military action from them as well as Iran. Make sure that Forts Wainright, Richardson, and Greely are all ready for a full-scale attack on the Kremlin if necessary. I know Camp Doha is ready, but alert them of the new players in the game. Our Japanese, Norway, and United Kingdom bases will have to join the party. I want the fleet that is currently in the Mediterranean to lock in coordinates on the closest Russian military bases. Also, activate Operation Ghost Town at Onizuka Air Station."

"Mr. President," chimed in Bryce Duncan, "Operation Ghost Town is a nuclear strike maneuver. You're talking world war here, and a nuclear war at that. This situation is not that grave."

"Thanks for the update, Bryce, but I am well aware of what Operation Ghost Town is. That is why it was named Ghost Town. The

United States was just threatened by a superpower and its lap dog. I plan to be prepared for both. I pray that we never have to go into war with anyone, especially a nuclear war, but I will use everything at my disposal to protect our country and its citizens. As far as the gravity of the situation, I tend to disagree. Our citizens are being threatened and killed by a foreign government. I can't think of a more legitimate reason to go to war."

"But sir," said Duncan, "the involvement of a foreign government has not been proven. All we know is that this is the action of a handful of terrorists acting independently."

"Of course, Moscow is the immediate target of Operation Ghost Town," said Patton, ignoring Duncan's last statement. "I want a full-scale attack on Karbala. Give them plenty of advance warning ahead of time. I want the citizens to be able to evacuate, but I want the city annihilated. Do not harm any of their religious shrines or Islamic schools. Inform them that if they are unable to leave the city before the bombing starts, they will be safe in their Islamic schools. Iraq and the terrorists must understand that every time our people are killed, it will come back on them tenfold. I want to strike Karbala as soon as my television appearance has ended. Have Operation Ghost Town operable at least fifteen minutes before I go on the air. If Russia or Iran comes to Iraq's aid, we will go for the jugular. Operation Ghost Town will be implemented only on my direct command. Is there anything else, Bryce?"

"Just one more thing, Mr. President," said Bryce.

"And that is?"

"Shall we notify your wife that her mother has been killed, or will you?"

The two men made unusually long eye contact. Patton had put that picture out of his mind and was now being forced to deal with it. It hurt, like salt being poured into an open wound. He knew Bryce did not agree with his strategy and was letting him know without being defiant. None-the-less, Patton did not like him very much at that moment.

"Katie is my responsibility; I will take care of it. If Katherine is indeed dead, the terrorists have made a big mistake, because they will have lost the leverage they thought they had. If she is alive, she still has a chance, albeit a very slim chance, to make it back home alive, because they will try to use her as the carrot to control us."

"They want us to believe that she may still be alive," said Bryce. "Then later, when we discover she is indeed dead, it will totally demoralize us. The stakes are getting higher, Mr. President. Can we still afford to play?"

"If the stakes are too high for you, Bryce, throw your hand in and fold. Was that a resignation?"

"No sir, it wasn't."

"Then everyone get back to work. Wake up Tommy and Darrin and bring them up to speed."

CHAPTER SEVENTEEN

A small six-passenger plane landed on private property in Langley, Virginia. The twin-engine craft taxied to a smooth stop. Its only passenger stepped out into the early morning darkness. A gray ford Taurus was parked a hundred feet from the door of the aircraft. A small building, two hundred yards in the distance, was the only other man-made thing in sight.

"Refuel the plane and wait for me here," commanded Dooley.

He slammed the door of the aircraft and headed for the vehicle. The plane taxied in the direction of the small building off in the distance. Dooley jumped into the car and buckled up. The key was already in the ignition. He started the vehicle and sped off in the opposite direction of the plane. Within minutes, he came to a country road. Turning left onto the road, Dooley accelerated as if time were against him. Reaching into the right pocket of his coat, he pulled out his cell phone. Steering with his left hand, and dialing with his right, he held the phone at eye level so he could watch the road and phone simultaneously.

"I will be there in fifteen minutes. Don't keep me waiting," Dooley said, ending the call and returning the phone to his pocket.

Thirteen minutes later, he pulled up to a small diner. Two men in dark single-breasted suits, brimmed hats and trench coats, exited the diner and got into the car. Bruce McAllister, carrying a small duffle bag, climbed into the back seat. John Conklin sat up front next to Dooley. John and Mac (as Bruce was called) were CIA operatives who were more loyal to Dooley than Pitts. Both of them owed their lives to him, and Dooley made sure they would never forget it. They had not served under Dooley. They had served in another unit that had worked with Dooley on a joint mission. They had not come across a building or security system they could not disarm..

"So is our buddy still a creature of habit?" asked Dooley.

"Of course," said Mac.

"Yeah, he still likes to get to the office a couple of hours before everyone else," added John.

"Good," said Dooley, let's have breakfast with good ole Nick."

After fifteen minutes of driving, the open countryside morphed into an affluent suburb. After a few miles, the nice houses were replaced by office buildings, commercial real estate, and retail outlets. Again, buildings became a rare sight as CIA Headquarters could be seen in the distance. The vehicle turned and headed for the massive structure.

"Is everything set as we discussed it?" asked Dooley. "No one is to see me coming or going."

"Don't worry, General," said John, "we have top clearance. There are so many secret entrances and exits we could hide you in there for a week without you ever being seen."

"An hour or so is all the time I'll need."

A couple of miles before reaching the CIA building, John and Dooley exchanged seats. John knew how to approach the building without being seen and without setting off any alarms. Dawn was ninety minutes away, and Dooley planned to be in and out before that first ray of sunlight pierced the darkness. John reached into the breast pocket of his jacket, pulled out a key, and handed it to Dooley.

"This might come in handy," he said.

Dooley's eyes sparkled as he grabbed the key. He almost smiled as he imagined the expression Pitts would have seeing him appear out of nowhere.

Bill Pitts sat in his office, staring into his computer. The light in his office was on, but the one in the outer office, where his assistant worked, was not. His office door was cracked open about three inches.

He liked to hear his assistant, Betty Hernandez, when she came in. He always had a list of things for her to start on first thing in the morning. She would usually come straight into his office and get her assignments, even before she removed her coat. Every morning, there was something he needed ten minutes ago.

As he pecked away on his keyboard, Pitts was oblivious that someone had entered his outer office. Dooley, John, and Mac had taken the utmost caution in being silent. All three had on surgical gloves. They had managed to enter the outer office, shut and lock the door behind them, and come within a step of Pitts's office door without making a sound. With his right hand, Dooley removed his pistol from a shoulder holster. His left hand was simultaneously removing a silencer from the left pocket of his trousers. With the skill and speed of someone who had done this hundreds of times, he connected the two.

"Is that you Betty?" asked Pitts, as he heard soft muffled sounds near his door.

Dooley pushed the door open and quickly walked in. He pointed his pistol at Pitts's forehead. John and Mac followed him into the room.

"Keep your hands where I can see them," said Dooley, as he walked around behind Pitts. "By the way, don't bother trying to set off the silent alarm. It has already been disconnected. I see you are still living up to your nickname. You cut yourself shaving again, didn't you?"

"So that's why you call him Nick," said Mac.

"Yes, and it will make our job much easier."

Pitts closed his eyes and pressed his lids shut very tightly for a second or two before opening them back up. He looked around the room and looked each man in the face. He looked them up and down as if he was trying to remember every detail about them. He looked at every weapon, bag, and item they pulled out.

"I can see how you got in here," said Pitts, looking at John and Mac. "What do you want? Why are you holding a gun on me?"

"I think you know why we're here," said Dooley. "Now listen very carefully because I will not repeat myself. Stand up very slowly, put on your suit jacket, and sit back down."

"Why?" asked Pitts?

Dooley shoved his pistol hard into the back of Pitts's head. Pitts did as he was told. Mac sat his bag down and opened it. He pulled out duct tape and a rope and handed both to John. John taped Pitts's wrists to the arms of the chair. Then he tied Pitts to his high-back chair. Meanwhile, Mac walked over and ripped the Band-Aid from Pitts's face, balled it up and threw it in his bag. This opened the cut as he knew it would.

"We wouldn't want any rope burns now, would we?" Dooley asked sarcastically,

"What in the hell is going on, Stewart? What is this all about?"

"You know what this is about, Nick. I offered to work with you. Instead, you set me up. You should know me well enough to know I would not just sit back and do nothing."

"Set you up? What are you talking about?"

"You should have taken acting classes. You're not very convincing playing the dumb blond. You're not even blond. Putting my calling card on that idiot was really a dumb move. You might as well had lifted my driver's license and put it in his pocket. I figured you to be smarter than that Nick."

"You don't actually think you can get away with murder right here in headquarters, do you?"

"Of course, I can," Dooley said, in a nonchalant manner. "Shut him up."

John pulled a large handkerchief from his coat and covered Pitts's mouth. He was careful not to tie it too tight. He did not want to leave any marks across Pitts's face. Mac reached into his bag and removed a small case. He opened it to reveal a syringe accompanied by a small bottle containing a clear liquid. He inserted the syringe into the bottle and withdrew the liquid until the syringe was full.

"I guess I should explain to you what is about to happen," said Dooley. "However, I am pretty sure you have a good idea. See, Mac here is going to inject this magic potion into that small cut on your face. Now everyone knows you have a habit of cutting yourself shaving, so no one will think anything about it. Don't worry; we even brought the same brand of bandages you use to cover it up. Anyway, this magic potion will take you out in about twenty minutes. Now listen to this, you will love this part. This stuff attacks your heart and has the same symptoms as cardiac arrest. That's right, Nick, you guessed it. The medical report will read that you died of a heart attack. The beautiful thing about this whole plan is that this wonderful potion is undetectable after six hours. In fact, it is damn near undetectable anyway, unless you are looking for it specifically. Oh, by the way, Betty is having some car problems. She will be arriving late this morning. She asked me to give you the message," said Dooley breaking out in laughter.

Dooley motioned to John and Mac. John walked around behind the bound man, grabbed hold of his head, and held it still. Placing his left hand on Pitts' face, Mac held it steady as he injected the clear liquid into the small cut on his jawbone. Pitts grimaced, more so because of his helpless predicament than the pain of the injection. John released his hold on Pitts's face and returned to the opposite side of the desk, as did Dooley. Mac removed a rag from his bag, cleaned his needle, and neatly packed it away. Dooley unscrewed the silencer from his pistol and put them both away as Mac placed a bandage over the small cut.

"Relax, Nick, I had thought about making your death more painful, but I came to my senses and decided to make it look as natural as possible."

Dooley looked at his watch. He sat in a chair next to the door and waited, never removing his eyes from Pitts. At the thirteen-minute mark, sweat began to trickle down Bill Pitts's face. His color began to fade.

"Untie him," ordered Dooley.

John and Mac removed the duct tape and rope, and Mac stuffed them into his bag. Pitts leaned his head back against his chair, eyeballed Dooley, and smiled. Two minutes later, he clutched his chest. Instinct forced him to fight for every breath. The pain in his chest became evident on his face. Suddenly lunging forward and with his eyes bulging, Pitts knocked paper, pens, and files from his desk. His left arm flailed aimlessly, knocking more items to the floor, as the fingers of his right hand looked as if they would puncture the left side of his chest. Mouth wide open, Pitts gasped for air. The sounds he uttered resembled a baby seal. Thirty seconds later, the right side of his face met his desk, and the struggle was over.

"What was that smile all about?" asked Mac.

"Who cares?" said Dooley. "Maybe he heard his mama talking to him before he went. I should snatch that glass eye out of his head and keep it as a souvenir, but that would kill the whole heart attack theory. Let's get out of here."

John and Mac inspected the room, making sure no evidence of their presence would be left behind. Dooley took one last look at Pitts before he left.

CHAPTER EIGHTEEN

Patton had been sitting for over an hour, contemplating the best way to break the news to Katie. Should he call her now and tell her, or should he let her sleep a little while longer before he gave her the bad news? In all likelihood, she had not slept at all since the plane was taken hostage. There was no best way. It would not make a difference how she was told or from whom she received the information. Bad news is bad news. The death of a parent, especially such a horrible death, is never received well. He picked up a cordless phone and made the call. The line rang twice before it was answered.

"Hello, Dale," answered Katie, sounding alert, as if she had been expecting the call.

"How are you holding up Katie?"

"You didn't call me this time of morning to ask me how I was holding up. This is the call I have been dreading, isn't it?"

"I am truly sorry Katie."

"When did you get the news?"

"Three hours ago. I guess I just didn't want to believe it."

"What exactly didn't you want to believe? Tell me what happened."

"Another tape was sent to us. It showed Katherine with a gun to her head. The film went black, and a split-second later a gunshot was heard. We can't actually confirm her death, but we believe that is just a terrorist ploy."

"In other words, you don't want me to have any hope of Mother being alive?"

"Katie, you know that's not true. You don't know how much this has been eating at me. You haven't seen the tape of innocent people being shot and killed like they were rabid animals. These are people who had already been beaten and bloodied. The gun was put to your mother's head just like the others. I have to believe her fate was the same."

"You're doing more than just believing, Dale; you're hoping she's dead. You never liked Mother. You two never got along."

"That's not true, I like your mother. Yes, we cut up, but we had an understanding. There was no real strife between us. She did not blame me for her situation, so why are you?"

"What are you talking about? How do you know that she didn't blame you?"

"I know because when she was facing the camera, she winked into it. She knew I would see the tape, and she winked at me. Katie, you know that's her way of apologizing or saying she is okay. She would never come out and say she was sorry or she was wrong, but she would wink instead. You know I'm right. You do it on occasion yourself. You got it from your mother."

Katie paused for a moment. She knew he was right. This did not ease the pain of the loss of her mother, but it did ease her anger against her husband. Katie was hurting too bad to just let it go. She said the first thing that came to her mind.

"How do I know you're not just saying that to get out of the doghouse?"

"Katie, you know I never lie to you, no matter how painful it is. I can't imagine you hearing anything more painful than what you have just heard.

Damn, he was right again. In all of her years of knowing him, Katie had never known him to lie to her. He was doing a good job of calming her down, but she did not want to calm down. At that moment she needed somebody to blame. She had to get off the phone, because she was about to burst into tears.

"Good night, Mr. President" she said, ending the call.

The connection was broken. A dial tone echoed in the president's ear. He turned off the cordless phone and returned it to its base. A moment later, he picked the phone back up and hurled it across the room. It smashed against the wall. Bobby, never out of earshot, kicked the door open with his pistol drawn. He saw the president standing in the middle of the floor with his back to him. After a quick look around, Bobby surmised what had happened. He holstered his pistol and left the room, gently closing the door behind him. Bobby heard a few more things hit the wall, and the sound of objects breaking continued for another five minutes. Four agents rounded the corner and came running down the hall. Bobby intercepted them and assured them that everything was fine. Moments later, all was quiet once again, but the silence was not peaceful.

Katie was not faring any better. All of the anger she had embraced hours earlier turned into grief that she could not contain. She cried until the sun peeked through her window. Her eyes were bloodshot and her throat was sore. The pillow, which she had clutched so tightly, was drenched. She had buried her face in it most of the night. Her blankets were on the floor. She had kicked them there in a fit of rage resembling a spoiled child having a temper tantrum. She quit from sheer exhaustion and actually managed to get an hour of sleep, which was more unsettling than relaxing.

The ring of the phone startled Katie from a semiconscious state. The news she had heard hours earlier echoed in her head. For a moment she believed it had all been a horrible nightmare. She looked at the phone as it rang for the fourth time. If she didn't answer it, she wouldn't hear any bad news. She put the pillow over her head, but it did not help. The constant ringing and flashbacks from her previous phone call brought tears to her already bloodshot eyes. Curling up in the fetal position, Katie pressed the pillow over her ears. After several minutes, the ringing finally stopped. She remained curled up in a ball and was about to doze off when she was interrupted again. This time, it was a knock at her bedroom door.

"Katie, Katie, are you all right?" asked Emily, raising her voice to be heard on the other side of the door?

"Go away," was Katie's reply.

Emily opened the door and took a few steps inside the room.

"Why didn't you answer your wakeup call? Are you ill? You know you have a speaking engagement in a little over an hour."

"Cancel it," ordered Katie.

"I can't do that; we have rescheduled it twice already. It is not a long engagement. You can be back here in a couple of hours. You only have to speak for about thirty minutes. Besides, you will be talking to one of your favorite groups, The Geritol Committee."

The Geritol Committee was a local senior citizen group, which supported many issues concerning the elderly. The group championed things like affordable health care and cleaner, safer conditions in nursing homes. The Committee enjoyed some local success but was pushing for national recognition. They were thrilled the first lady supported them. She could give them the presence they needed to expand nationally.

"Come on, Katie, those people are counting on you. You won't find a bigger support group, and you really believe in their cause."

"You're right," said Katie, tossing her pillow aside. "We can't keep putting them off. Besides, Mom was a member of the Geritol Committee."

"Don't talk like that. There is still hope for Ms. Katherine."

Katie pulled herself to the edge of the bed, with her back to Emily. She turned and looked at Emily for a few moments, then turned her head back around and looked down at the floor.

"Oh my God, you have heard something, haven't you? Is Ms. Katherine okay?"

"She is fine now," Katie whispered softly.

Emily put her hands to her mouth, as her eyes filled with tears. She took a few steps toward the bed and leaned against it, more to steady her balance than to comfort Katie. She took a few more steps forward and placed her right hand on Katie's left shoulder. She squeezed it a few times as if she was massaging it.

"I am so sorry Katie. When did you get the news?"

"Last night, actually early this morning is more accurate. Please stop crying. I have cried enough tears to launch a ship. My eyes are blood red, I'm exhausted and weak from crying all night, and I am due to speak in about an hour. Well, I guess that is what eye drops and makeup are for. Will you get me some juice and toast? I will be ready in about forty minutes."

"Sure," said Emily as she managed a smile. "Anything else I can do for you?"

"Just be there to catch me when I fall."

"No need, the moon will drop from the sky before you fall."

Patton had not been back to sleep since he had viewed the second tape. The last few seconds of the tape, followed by his conversation with Katie, played over and over again in his head. He was in new territory; he had never experienced anything like this. Never before had his home been affected by anything he did outside of it. He could feel his emotions going up and down, as if he was on some carnival ride. When he appeared to have his normal rock-steady demeanor, the situation would take a sharp turn, chipping away at the rock. After much thought, a half-smile came across his face. He would handle it the only way he knew how. He was being tested. The enemy was waiting for him to crack. The enemy would have a long wait.

Patton did a self-evaluation. He took his family out of the equation and questioned his every decision, for the last time. He was satisfied with his answer because he determined that he would have made the exact same decisions had his family not been involved. The enemy had made it tough, but they were dealing with him at full mental capacity. This is what made him smile. At that moment, Patton decided he would never second-guess himself again. These terrorists had picked the wrong person to anger, and he would make sure they remembered it. His thoughts were suddenly interrupted by a knock at the door.

"It's open," he said.

Bobby came in and said, "The First Lady has just left for her speaking engagement.

"How was she?"

"I am told she is holding up well. I was informed that she did look a little tired."

"When did the news break?"

"Approximately an hour ago," said Bobby. "Don't worry Dale. Katie knows what she is up against."

"I know she knows. I just hope she can handle it."

"Well, buddy, she's learned from the best, so may the Lord have mercy on whoever crosses her. Katie will be fine. You need to worry about yourself. I heard I may have to pull Harry Graham off of you this morning."

Harry Graham was the Speaker of the House. He was the President's first meeting this morning. He was meeting with Patton about the way he was handling the hijacking of AWA Flight 454. Patton knew he had taken a few liberties, but he had hoped to have the proof of Iraq's involvement by now. He also knew he couldn't expect any help from the gentleman from Kentucky, who had a reputation for having more party loyalty than sense. The Democrats referred to him as Speaker No, because he always found fault with any Democrat-sponsored bill or idea, no matter how good and beneficial it was. Patton had heard all of the rumors, including those about impeachment. He knew Speaker Graham would be the first one in line to start the impeachment process and that this meeting was another test of the new President. The Speaker from Kentucky did not know what a worthy and powerful adversary the president was.

"It's not going to be pretty," Patton said, "but it won't come to that. He will talk. I will listen, and then we both will do what we had planned before the meeting."

"Well," said Bobby, "you know what you're up against. It sounds as if you're going to follow protocol just to get through it so that you can get back to work."

"That's exactly right," said Patton.

"Are you ready to face Speaker No?"

"Sure," said Patton, "let's get this over with."

A few moments later, Patton, Bobby, and two other security officers escorted the president to a small, private lounge. The president could not enter until Bobby gave it a thorough search. Speaker Graham was already inside, waiting for the president. Bobby decided to irritate the Speaker by asking to see his identification. Begrudgingly, he pulled it out and handed it to Bobby without saying a word. After a quick walk-through, Bobby was convinced that the room was safe and left to allow the president to enter.

"Be careful, it's a little cool in there," said Bobby.

Patton smiled as he entered the room and closed the door behind him. He had never talked to Speaker Graham one on one before. He had watched him on television and even seen him across the room on a couple of occasions. Until now, neither person had made an attempt to greet the other. The Speaker was of average height and thin build and looked every bit of his seventy-two years. He was bald on top and had a pointed little nose that supported his wire-rim glasses. Speaker Graham stood and shook the president's hand as they exchanged a polite greeting.

"Thank you, Mr. Speaker, for meeting with me on such a short notice," said the President. "Under the circumstances, we both knew this meeting was inevitable."

"With all due respect, Mr. President, cut to the chase," replied Speaker Graham."

"Mr. Speaker, you know exactly why I asked you here," said Patton. "The republicans control Congress, and you seem to control the republicans. I need Congress to declare Iraq's part in the hijacking as an act of war."

"I thought Congress had already made that declaration based on your television response to the perpetrators," said the Speaker, peering over the top of his glasses.

"Harry, don't mistake this meeting for something that it's not. A minute ago, you instructed me to cut to the chase and I did. Now, I am instructing you to stop playing games. I laugh and joke, but I do not play. This meeting is merely protocol f or me, nothing more. There is nothing you can say to convince me to change my course of action. However, protocol dictates that I address congress, and that's where you come in."

"As you wish," said the Speaker in a very cold tone. "The majority of Congress feels as I do. You, Mr. President, are acting irrationally. There is no evidence that Iraq is behind the hijacking and murders. Therefore, there is no reason to declare their actions as an act of war. As tough as it may be, we need to double our efforts in enlisting Iraq's help to bring our citizens home. I have been instructed to inform you that if your aggressiveness against Iraq does not cease immediately, Congress will take steps toward impeachment. Those efforts have to be made clear in tonight's reply to the terrorists. If not, the matter of your impeachment will be brought to the floor when Congress convenes on Monday, and the House Judiciary Committee will proceed with the impeachment process."

"That's about what I expected," said Patton. "Are you saying Congress would be willing to make that declaration if it had proof Iraq was directly involved?"

"I am saying that could possibly help you keep your job a little while longer. Do you have proof?"

"Thank you for your time, Mr. Speaker, and enjoy your day," Patton said as he turned and headed for the door.

Harry Graham's face turned bloody red as he watched the president walk out. He felt as if he had been slapped in the face. This was how he treated people, not how they treated him. The Speaker didn't know how to react. He sheepishly looked around the room, even though he knew no one else was present. Apparently the President did not know who he was dealing with, he thought. He would learn, and learn quickly.

"You were right," said Bobby, as he, Patton, and the rest of the security team walked the President down the hall. "It didn't last more than fifteen minutes, more like five minutes."

"He was pretty much what I pictured him to be. He's easy to figure out. His main goal is to cause me as much trouble as he can and discredit me at every opportunity. Let's get back to work."

Everyone met back in the war room. General Phillips, Bryce Duncan, John Clermont, and Bobby were all waiting patiently as the President finished his conversation with the vice president. Patton was getting a little frustrated. His conversation with Speaker Graham didn't help. He wanted the proof of Iraq's involvement more than ever. He wasn't afraid of being impeached. He was a fierce competitor and hated the idea of anyone giving him an ultimatum or forcing his hand. He was like all warriors: when you back them in a corner, they come out fighting, and directly in front of them is the last place you want to be.

"I'm checking on some hunches," said Darrin, "but no conclusive evidence yet. I have watched both tapes about a hundred times. There is something about them, especially the first one, that seems oddly familiar, but I can't put my finger on it."

"I need that proof Darrin. That asshole from Kentucky would like nothing better than to bring me up on charges. I know I can deem this incident as a state of emergency and exercise my powers as commander-in-chief, but I would rather have Congress declare Iraq's involvement as an act of war instead of me pulling rank. I don't think a state-of-emergency decision would hold up without that proof."

"We still have a couple of days before all hell breaks loose. By then, I should be able to figure out what I'm overlooking."

"You mean Iraq only has a couple of days before all hell breaks loose," said Patton.

"Right now, our fate is tied to Iraq's," said Darrin. "We could both lose. Did you hear about Bill Pitts?"

"What about him?"

"He was found dead in his office this morning."

"What happened to him?"

"Preliminary investigations point to a massive coronary, but the investigation is ongoing. He was found by his secretary. She has been so distraught that they haven't been able to get anything out of her. Rumor is that Pitts had some type of surveillance device, but nobody knows what it is. His secretary was the only person he trusted. If he had a surveillance device, she would know about it. The FBI wants to talk to her and look at surveillance tapes, if they exist, before the cause of death is documented."

"Why is the FBI involved in what appears to be a heart attack?"

"Two reasons," said Darrin. "First, he was the CIA Director. His position alone would draw the FBI's interest. Second, if Pitts's death wasn't caused by a massive coronary, then it was an inside job. The man was in his office in one of the most secure buildings in the world. Not only would it take someone with knowledge of the building's security, but they would have to know how to manipulate it."

"Interesting," commented the president. "Keep me updated on that situation. In the meantime, your main priority is to get me proof of Iraq's involvement in this hijacking. Let me know the minute you have something."

"I'm on it, Mr. President."

Patton turned the phone off and handed it to Bobby, who took it and returned to his station. The president paused in thought for few moments as everyone's eyes were fixed on him.

"It seems that things are getting more interesting by the minute," said Patton. Not only do we not have conclusive proof yet of Iraq's involvement in this situation, but CIA Director Bill Pitts was found dead in his office this morning. The initial indication is that he died from a heart attack, but an investigation is being conducted."

"No big loss," said Bryce, "one less creep looking over your shoulder."

"I'm surprised you feel that way. I thought Pitts was someone you looked up to."

Bryce knew the President wasn't complimenting him. It was just the opposite. Patton was letting him know he was still on the outside looking in. He was a long way off from being one of his trusted advisors. Bryce figured he would be replaced after the hijacking situation had been resolved. He decided not to let it bother him. He had nothing against the president but wasn't afraid to speak his mind. The president had the wrong person if he wanted a yes-man.

"I don't know of anyone who looked up to Pitts."

"Okay gentlemen," said the president, "I need some status reports. Will everything be ready by the time I go on the air this evening?"

"Yes sir," said General Phillips. Duncan and I have briefed the Joint Chiefs of Staff. They assure us that everything will be ready and in place at least an hour before you are scheduled to go on the air."

"As we speak," said Bryce, "coordinates for Operation Ghost Town are being calculated, and military units are moving into position."

"Our diplomatic efforts have been in vain," said Clermont. "Iraq, Iran, and Russia have not changed their positions."

"Do they understand the situation?" asked the President.

"Yes," said Clermont. "Our position was communicated to them in no uncertain terms."

"Good," said Patton. "Contact the Department of Commerce and cancel all exports to Iraq and Iran, effective immediately. That includes anything in route."

"Consider it done, sir," said Clermont. "What about Russia?"

"Contact all countries bordering Iran and Russia and warn them to prepare for possible nuclear fallout. Explain the situation to them and make it clear this is the only warning they are likely to get. Give the heads of state an approximate time of when I will go on the air and tell them nuclear fallout will depend on Iran's and Russia's interference in American affairs. There will be no advanced warning other than this. Iran has been threatening nuclear capabilities for years. We may soon find out whether they actually have it. Assure them that the United States will aid in any collateral damage."

"You can't be serious," said Bryce.

"Mr. President, you could be starting a nuclear war just by sending that message," blurted General Phillips.

"Gentlemen, starting a war with anyone is never my intent, but I will not run from one if it means abandoning our citizens. Innocent Americans are dying before our eyes while we sit here in meetings arguing the best course of action. Past protocol dictates we try a little diplomacy and try to negotiate and reason with the animals responsible for these heinous acts. Well, I am establishing a new protocol. Any country that threatens or harms our citizens will face the full wrath of the US military. Believe me, I am not crazy, and I am not acting irresponsibly or out of revenge. I have given this a lot of thought, and my decisions are not off the cuff. I need to know right now if any of you want out."

All of them looked at Patton in disbelief, but no one said anything. Bryce held back a grin. He loved it, even though he had to be the voice of reason sometimes. This was the first time he felt as if he really wanted to be a part of this administration. He broke the silence.

"It looks as if everyone is on board. If that is all, Mr. President, I need to get to work."

"I want status reports from each of you thirty minutes before I go on the air. We're not starting a war; we're preventing one."

General Phillips, Bryce, and Clermont got up and left the room. Patton allowed a half smile to cross his face for a few seconds. He was starting to understand Bryce Duncan, but he wasn't sold on him just yet.

CHAPTER NINETEEN

As Bill Pitts's corpse lay across his desk, half a dozen FBI agents moved around like worker ants. Ray Silva led the investigation. He felt that the investigation of the top person in the CIA should be spearheaded by the top person in the FBI, even if the death was due to natural causes. He had no great love for Pitts, but he respected his work. Ray Silva was already wondering who would be the next CIA Director.

Pitts's assistant, Betty Hernandez, sat in a corner chair looking disheveled and sounding a bit incoherent. She appeared to be mumbling to herself when the FBI Director approached her. Betty was the youngest child of Mexican immigrants. She was the only one of her siblings born in the United States. Her full name was Betty Davis Hernandez; she was named after the American movie star. She loved the name Betty Davis and only used her last name when she legally had to.

"Ms. Hernandez, tell me what happened," Silva said.

Betty seemed to be unaware of Silva's presence. She was still mumbling under her breath.

"Ms. Hernandez!" Silva said, raising his voice.

Silva startled Betty, and she jumped.

"Calm down, calm down," Silva said, as he made eye contact with her. "Tell me what happened to your boss."

Betty glanced over at Pitts, and her eyes started to water. She began to cry. She turned back to Silva and started telling her account of the situation.

"Whoa, whoa," said Silva. "English, speak to me in English."

"I'm sorry. I do that sometimes when I am upset."

"It's okay. Just relax and tell me what you know."

"I don't know anything. He was like that when I got to work this morning. I got to work later than usual because I had car trouble. I had two flat tires. I can't remember the last time I had a flat tire, and this morning I had two. Anyway, when I got here, I rushed right into Bill's office. He always has something he needs me to do right away, and I figured he would be upset with me because I was late. When I came in, I found him just like he is now. I ran back to my desk and hit the silent alarm. Security showed up in no time. The next thing I know, you and the rest of the bureau were here."

"Do you know of any medical conditions that Mr. Pitts had?"

"No, he very rarely talked about his personal life. He always said he had a lot of enemies and that I was the only one he could trust."

"Was someone after him?"

"Let Bill tell it; somebody was always after him. For the last five years, he has been saying that he doubts if he will make it to the end of the year. A few years ago, he invested in some type of high-tech security system. He told me to always remember two things. First, if I ever heard that he was dead, no matter how innocent it may appear, I was never to believe it was anything other than murder. Second, he would say the truth is in the eyes."

"From all indications, it looks as if Pitts died from a heart attack. The medical examiner said as much in his preliminary examination. According to what you just said, we should be looking for another cause of death."

"Maybe you should start by looking in his eye," said Betty.

"What is that supposed to mean?"

"You know Bill had a glass eye, don't you?"

"Of course, I do. His left eye is false. That's how he got his nickname, Eagle Eye."

"True, but that nickname took on a whole new meaning."

"What are you talking about," said Silva?

"I never knew what Bill meant when he would say the truth is in the eyes until he explained it to me about six months ago. He actually meant the truth would be in his eye, his glass eye. The new security system he told me about is a small camera in his glass eye that he can record from. He activates it by closing his eye and pressing his eyelid against it. He turns it on and off that way."

"Well, I'll be damned," said Silva.

Silva walked over to Pitts, bent down, and looked at his face. He took his right hand and raised Pitts's left eyelid. He moved in a little closer to get a better look.

"There is something going on in there," said Silva. "Technology never ceases to amaze me. Ms. Hernandez, can I yank that eyeball right out without screwing it up?"

"I have no idea," she said.

"I better play it safe. I'll have the coroner do a full evaluation and make sure he is extra careful in removing that eye."

Silva released Pitts' eyelid and stood up straight. He walked back over to Betty.

"Is there anything else about Pitts that I should know?"

"Nothing that I can think of."

"You better go on home," said Silva, "but stay close to the phone in case I need to talk to you."

"Yes sir, I will do that," said Betty. "Will you let me know if Bill died from anything other than a heart attack?"

"I will let you know what I can."

The news of the CIA director's death spread quickly. Phones throughout DC, Maryland, and Virginia were ringing off the hook. Dooley sat at his desk, listening intently. He held a cell phone to his right ear and listened to the person on the other end with a patience he seldom showed. His facial expressions indicated that each spoken word was of extreme importance. With a creased brow and pursed lips, Dooley continued to listen. His focus and complete attention was on the caller. After a few moments, all the blood drained from his face.

Dooley turned pale and ghostly looking. He put his left hand up to his forehead and continued to listen.

When the call ended, Dooley placed the phone on the edge of his desk. He stared at it as if he expected it to ring again, as if he expected the person to call back and tell him the previous conversation was all a sick joke. Dooley knew Pitts was dead before the phone rang. However, he didn't know about the camera in Pitts's eye. He wished he had snatched that glass eye and kept it as a souvenir like he wanted to do. Now he knew why Pitts had smiled at them. Pitts's body was in the custody of the FBI. It would be impossible to get his eye now. "Damn him!" said Dooley as his bald head started to glisten with sweat. "How could I not have known about that damn eye?"

Dooley racked his brain, trying to figure out how he could get himself out of this mess. He had been in tough situations before. He just needed to think. Who did he know in the FBI who would help him? Was there someone in the Coroner's office that owed him a favor? A high- ranking CIA agent could be just as useful. Dooley kept coming up blank. There has to be somebody who could get the eye for him.

"Think, General, think," he commanded himself. "If I can't snatch the eye, there has to be a way to ruin the picture without having it in my hand. This could be a job for an ambitious techie."

Sweat had started to roll down Dooley's face. He had to wipe his furrowed brow every few moments to keep the sweat out of his eyes. He loosened his tie and unfastened his collar button. He leaned forward and hit the button on his intercom.

"Rachel, take the rest of the day off," he said.

"Senator," Rachel answered, "are you feeling okay? You hardly ever give me a day off."

"Then I guess it's time," said Dooley. "I have some concerns that will tie me up all day, so you might as well take the day off."

"No problem, I'm on my way out the door before you change your mind. Thanks, Senator."

Dooley turned off the intercom and leaned back in his chair. He continued to rack his brain for a solution to his predicament. He would call his accomplices. They had a technology background and had worked in security before becoming full operatives. They were in as deep as he was. Hopefully, they could come up with a solution. If Pitts's body was still in the building, they could get to it. This was his best chance. He picked his phone and dialed a number. The line seemed to ring forever before anyone answered.

"I can't talk long. What's up?" answered Mac.

"Have you heard the news about Pitts?" Dooley asked.

"You must be getting too old for this type of work. Our agents and the FBI are swarming around here like bees. You better keep it together. I have to go."

"Wait a minute, you idiot," said Dooley. "I'm not talking about his death. I'm talking about the camera Pitts had in his fake eye."

"What the hell are you talking about?"

"A reliable source informed me that Pitts had a video camera installed in his fake eye. He basically just had to blink his eyes hard to activate it. That's why he was smiling before he died."

"If this is a double cross big guy, I will…"

"This isn't a damn double cross," said Dooley. "This is real."

"Why the hell didn't you know about this? You have top clearance on all personnel records."

"I knew about the eye. I didn't know about the camera. That is something it seems only his assistant knew about. You need to brief John, and the two of you have to find a way to get, or deactivate that eye."

"That explains a lot," said Mac.

"Exactly what does that explain?"

"Pitts's body was moved to a medical unit here in the building and put under twenty-four-hour guard. That came straight from Silva. We were informed that he is going to bring someone in to do an autopsy instead of sending the body out, and a surveillance camera will be on the body around the clock. Silva has to know about the eye camera."

"You and John will have to find a way, and quick. Our lives depend on it."

"You're asking the impossible, Dooley, especially on such short notice. Someone will be here within the hour to start the autopsy, and you know the eye will be the first thing removed and handed to Silva. John and I will probably leave the country. I suggest you do the same. Good luck."

Mac hung up. Dooley heard the click of the phone just as he was about to respond. Dooley called Mac's name a few times, to no avail. According to Mac, he may have a couple of hours at most before the secrets of the eye were disclosed. Dooley ended the connection and set his phone back on the desk.

This was all wrong thought Dooley. This was not how he was supposed to go out. First the president had threatened to bring murder charges against him if he didn't resign, and now this. He could fight the president's accusations, but how could he fight video evidence of him participating in a murder? Dooley surmised that he wouldn't be in this predicament if it wasn't for the president. Dale Patton was the root of all his problems.

"Damn you, Dale! You weren't supposed to come back from Iraq on that last mission."

Dooley glanced around the room until he spotted his dress blues, which were lying across the arm of a chair. He had planned to wear them tonight to critique the President's second response to the hijacking. This was not the usual occasion for wearing his uniform, but he was known for doing the unusual once in a while. Besides, he had thought he would be commenting on military operations and tactics, so wearing a military uniform seemed to be in order. Michelle Mason had asked him to be on standby for this evening's telecast. He was sure he would get a call once the contents of the second tape were made known. The president was starting to look more and more vulnerable, and he wanted to be there when he cracked. Dooley knew he would not be there to witness that moment. He also knew he could not stand the idea of Patton gloating at him in prison.

Dooley got up from his chair and walked over to his dress blues. He picked up the uniform and removed it from the plastic. He started to change clothes right there in his office. He took his time and stripped down to his under clothes. He used a handkerchief he had removed from the pocket of his slacks to wipe the sweat from his head and face. He then took his time and put on each piece of his uniform. He paused every once in a while to remove a piece of lint or wipe down the material. He brushed at the red stripe on each pant leg before putting them on. When he got to his jacket, he took the time to shine and adjust each medal; there were many. He slowly buttoned each button. He smiled at how well his old uniform still fit him. Last but not least, he grabbed his hat and wiped the top of it before placing it on his head. He adjusted it to make sure it hung just right. He casually strolled back over to his desk and sat back down in the chair.

He sat straight up in the chair with his fingers interlocked in his lap and his elbows resting on the arms of the chair. He just sat there, staring straight ahead. At first he enjoyed the silence, and then his mind started to replay his life over the last eighteen months. Why didn't he win the presidency? He had bested Patton at everything else. He was his commanding officer. All of Patton's accomplishments were because of him. In actuality, they were in spite of him but that wasn't how he saw it. Even in defeat, life was still bearable until three days ago. That's when Patton summoned him to the Oval Office and ordered him to get out of town or else. He hadn't been ordered to do anything in almost twenty years. This was all Patton's fault.

Dooley opened the drawer in the middle of his desk. He removed his pistol and the silencer he kept with it. He slowly connected the two. He moved his cell phone to the side and placed his pistol in the center of his desk. He then spun the barrel and watched the pistol spin in a circle. It slowly came to a stop, with the barrel pointed straight at him. He spun the pistol again. This time when it stopped, the barrel pointed away from him, toward the door. Again, he spun the pistol, and again the barrel pointed at him when it stopped.

In one motion, Dooley grabbed the pistol by the handle, placed the barrel to his temple, and pulled the trigger. The impact of the bullet going through his head forced his head to the left, knocking his cap to the floor. The recoil from the shot forced the pistol in the opposite direction and out of his right hand. The pistol fell to the floor, still smoking. The bullet exited the left side of Dooley's head with great force, spraying blood and brains like a geyser. It left a hole large enough to stick a light bulb in. Dooley slumped over to his left. Blood and pieces of grey matter streamed from the exit wound, down what remained of the left side of his head and to his shoulder. It dripped from his shoulder and started to puddle on the floor. There was a small hole in the opposite wall where the bullet had lodged.

A few short moments later, the phone rang in the outer office. It rang four or five times before it went into voice mail. A few seconds after that, a red light blinked indicating that someone had left a message.

"That's one call I know will be returned," said Michelle Mason. "He would never pass up an opportunity to berate the President."

CHAPTER TWENTY

The Secret Service Agent held the door of the limousine open as Katie and Emily climbed into the back-seat. The silver haired members of the Geritol Committee waved from a distance. The limousine was sandwiched between the two black sedans, their security detail. As soon as the agent entered the car behind the limousine, the front car sped away, followed by the limousine and the trailing sedan.

Both women sat in silence as the cars maneuvered their way through traffic. Unaware that Emily was staring at her, Katie stared out the window, lost in thought. Still a bit overwhelmed, she tried to make sense of the last forty-eight hours. She had led a rather sheltered life. She had never faced adversity of this magnitude. Her father died when she was very young, and she barely remembered him. She was very close to her brother Thomas, but she and her mom were best of friends, especially during her teen years. Thomas ran a successful PR firm in San Francisco. Like her mother, he had left Washington right after the Inaugural Ball. He would be returning in the morning.

Katie thought about Dale's words, about her mother winking at the camera right before she died. She trusted Dale implicitly, but she had to see it for herself. Her mother's wink was always a calming influence for her. She decided that would be the first thing she did when she got back to the White House. Darrin would not refuse her. He and Bobby had known Katherine for a long time, and they had both witnessed her trademark wink. Sometimes it was a wordless apology, and other times it was a reassuring gesture.

"You're mighty quiet," said Emily. "Are you okay?"

"I'm coping," Katie said, as she turned to face Emily.

"You did very well. They loved you."

"Thank you. They were great. I'm glad I came. They actually made me forget about my own problems for a few minutes. You know Mother really loved and believed in that group."

"I know," said Emily. "I know, but don't talk about your mother in the past tense like that. From what you shared with me, there is no evidence that she is gone. She may still be alive. You have to believe."

"I do believe, Emily. I believe my mother is gone. I prayed on it. I prayed and cried all night, and do you know what God's reply was?"

"What was it?" Emily asked.

"It was the same thing that God told Paul when he asked for the thorn to be removed from his side."

Emily's eyes filled with water, for she knew the Bible as well as Katie. As hard as she tried to hold them back, the tears came. Emily removed a tissue from her purse and dabbed at her eyes.

"I didn't hear a booming voice, or even a whisper. However, the more I cried and begged for my mother's life, the more that passage of scripture came to mind. I thought I wasn't thinking straight, so I cried and begged some more. I tried to recall other passages that were more enlightening, but for the life of me I couldn't remember a single one. As many scripture passages as I know by heart, I couldn't remember any of them but that one; *My grace is sufficient.' 'My grace is sufficient'* is the only scripture that kept piercing my brain."

"I'm sorry," said Emily.

"Thank you, Emily but I'm okay. The strangest thing happened once I accepted that Mom was gone. I know it sounds corny, and you hear it all the time, but a strange peace came over me. In the midst of that peace, another scripture started to bounce around inside my head, and I can't get rid of it."

"This one has to be more reassuring than the first. Which one is it," asked Emily?

"I don't think reassurance is the main intent of this scripture. I think it's more instructional. The third chapter of Proverbs, verses 5 and 6 are the scriptures that are speaking to me now."

"I see what you mean," said Emily. *Trust in the Lord with all thine heart, and lean not unto your own understanding. In all thy ways acknowledge him, and he shall direct thy path.'* "That piece of scripture is very encouraging."

"It is encouraging, but at this point in time, it's also instructional. You see, that is Dale's favorite piece of scripture. I think God is telling me that I should be with my husband and be part of his support system, not a distraction."

"I'm going to be obedient, but first I need closure," said Katie.

"What kind of closure?" asked Emily.

"I have to see that last tape from the terrorists. Dale told me that mom winked into the camera. I have to see that. It's important to me."

"Katie, aren't you afraid that watching that tape will be more traumatizing than encouraging? I have heard that your mother was beaten and that she looked pretty bad. Can you handle looking at her in that condition?"

"I have to, and I will. That wink was her last communication to us, and I have to know that regardless of her situation, she was at peace when she died. It won't be any more difficult than sitting at her death bed with all kinds of tubes and wires hooked up to her, trying to listen to her last words."

"No, I guess not," said Emily.

"That will be the first thing I look into when we get back. Meanwhile, I want you to clear my schedule for the rest of the week and secure transportation to Camp David for me. I belong with my husband during times like these."

"I will take care of it," said Emily. "I am glad you're going to Camp David, but I'm not so sure watching that tape will do anything but upset you more."

"I appreciate your concern," said Katie, "but it's time I start acting like the first lady."

Katie turned back toward the window and once again became consumed in thought. She knew watching the tape would be difficult, but she had to do it. She hoped Darrin would understand and not try to talk her out of it. He could tell her it was classified and confidential information that she wasn't allowed to see, but she was pretty sure he wouldn't do that. The worst thing that could happen was if Katherine hadn't winked at all, if Dale had made the whole thing up to calm her down. No, she couldn't think that way. Her mind was playing tricks on her. Dale knew how close she and her Mother were. He wouldn't lie about something like that. That would be cruel, worse than cruel. Her sanity depended on seeing her mom wink one last time.

When the limousine stopped in front of the White House Katie, didn't wait for the Secret Service agents to open her door. She opened it herself, got out of the vehicle and walked swiftly to the door. Emily could not catch her. The Secret Service agents hurried to her side, but she was almost at the entrance before they caught up to her.

Emily followed behind alone and said sarcastically to herself, "Thanks guys, for escorting me in."

Katie made a beeline straight to her office. She dropped her coat into a chair just inside the door as she almost ran to her desk. Taking a seat and grabbing the phone at the same time, Katie called the vice president. She couldn't wait a moment longer. She had to see the wink for herself.

She waited patiently at her desk. What had seemed like hours had actually only been twenty minutes. What could be taking Darrin so long? She had informed Janet, her secretary, that he was on the way and had instructed her to allow him through without any delay. She even informed her not to make small talk with the vice president because his visit was of the utmost importance. Katie's eyes focused on the entrance as she heard footsteps coming her way.

"Sorry for the delay, Katie," said Darrin. "I came as quickly as I could. You know this tape is classified information. I had to exert a little authority to get it."

"Thank you," said Katie as she walked around the desk to greet Darrin. "This means a great deal to me."

"I gathered as much from the urgency in your voice. Are you sure you want to see this? Some of it can be pretty upsetting."

"I'm sure," said Katie. "I want to see the entire thing."

Darrin was carrying an unmarked DVD case with a disc inside. He walked over to the wall-mounted flat screen and pressed the eject button. He removed the disc from the case, inserted it into the extended holder, and closed it. He then walked over to the desk and picked up the remote.

"There are a few things I want to tell you about your mother before you watch this," he said. "This is for your ears only. There is no comprehensive proof at this time, but if your mother is gone, she died trying to save others."

"What are you talking about?" asked Katie.

"The hijackers noticed the security traveling with your mother and her friend. One of the agents was killed and the other badly wounded, but they didn't disclose the identity of your mother. They simply said their employers were wealthy American tourist. Katherine knew the terrorists didn't believe the agents. When she was asked who she was, she told them she was the president's mother. She drew the attention to her, and not for selfish reasons."

"Mom said that?"

"She most certainly did, and we believe she knew exactly what she was doing. When the terrorists found out she was the first mother-in-law, and not the First Mother, they made it hard on her and she was used as a pawn to get to Dale in more ways than one."

"I have been playing right into their hands, haven't I?" she asked.

"You have been a daughter concerned for her mother."

"I have been more than that. I have been an ass, blaming Dale for mother's plight. How did they find out her real identity?"

"They found out through the media," answered Darrin. "We believe there was a leak from within the White House. Tommy and I were blind-sided in that first press release about the hijacking. I don't think you realize how timely and how important your appearance at that press conference was. However, I thought you knew how close your mother and Dale are. They're like school kids who show their affection for one another by putting each other down and punching each other in the arm."

"Darrin, are you saying that Mother and Dale really liked each other?"

"That's exactly what I'm saying."

"How come I wasn't told about all of this, about Mother pretending to be Dale's mother?"

"As I said, this is confidential information. We're still looking for who the leak in the White House is. I am sure Dale would have told you once this was all over. I think he is feeling as bad as you. He feels he let your mother down. You see, Katie, Dale is pretty well known throughout the world for his military exploits. I think your mother felt a since of security by attaching herself to him. Her biggest mistake was that she underestimated the terrorists. The thing she thought would protect her most probably got her killed."

"I'm speechless. I don't know what to say. I'm ashamed of the way I have been acting. Dale deserves better. I should have known better."

"Dale's a big boy. He can take care of himself. His main concern is your physical and mental well-being. He's been through a few wars, but none of them have separated the two of you. He's praying this one doesn't do that either."

"It won't. I admit I took it pretty hard, and I did blame Dale for a lot of it. But Darrin, I swear to you I have never thought about leaving Dale."

"That's something Dale needs to hear. Watch the tape, Katie, and think back to the times Dale and your mother had their so-called spats. Think about the look in their eyes. You know the saying; the eyes are the windows to the soul. If they were really mad at each other, their eyes would have revealed it. All I ever saw was a twinkle in their eyes when they went at each other. They were enjoying themselves, and they understood each other. Even on this tape, there is no anger in your mother's eyes. She appears near the end of the tape. I will fast forward to her.

"No, don't do that. I want to see the entire tape. I want to watch it alone.

"As you wish," said Darrin. "The tape is not very long. I will go in here and chat with Janet while you watch it."

Darrin handed Katie the remote and walked into the outer office. When he left the room, Katie pressed the play button and sat down on the edge of her desk. She wasn't sure what to expect, but she knew she wouldn't like what she saw. Katie watched each agonizing minute with a steely resolve. She was determined not to shed any tears. The brutality of these people was more enlightening than frightening. The sheer disregard for human life actually made Katie angrier than anything else. No, it was beyond anger; it was hate. She was starting to realize why Dale had such strong feelings about dealing with terrorists.

The camera focused on Katherine, and Katie's resolve was severely challenged. She felt the tears come to her eyes, but she held them back. Her mother looked bad, but not as bad as her imagination had portrayed her. There it was! It was unmistakable. Dale should have told her about it sooner, she thought. Katie had a newfound respect for her mother. She actually risked her life for others. Katie new her mother had these selfless qualities, but soon the world would know that she had the presence of mind to communicate through a wink with everything she was going through. Katie's resolve went out the window as tears flowed down her cheeks, tears of joy and respect.

Katie walked into the outer office with the disc and handed it to Darrin.

"I need to get to Camp David ASAP," she told him. "Be a sweetheart and make it happen."

"Yes, ma'am," said Darrin, as Katie walked back into her office.

CHAPTER TWENTY-ONE

Michelle Mason picked lint from her blazer, played with her hair, and doubled-checked her microphone as she waited for her cue. Soon the cameras would be rolling, and she would be live, informing the world about the events of the past twenty-four hours, regarding the hijacking of AWA Flight 454. The president would follow with his second response to the terrorist actions. There was the cue; ten seconds before the live broadcast.

"Hello once again, I am Michelle Mason, and welcome to part two of the special report on the hijacking of AWA Flight 454. A lot has taken place in the last twenty-four hours that you don't want to miss. Don't go away, I'll be right back."

The president was in the war room with his advisors. John Clermont, Bryce Duncan, General Phillips, and Bobby were all present. Tommy had been flown in early that morning at the President's request. He had been summoned to join the inner circle and was on cloud nine. He was about to burst with enthusiasm, but he kept it well hidden from everyone but the ever- watchful eyes of Bobby Parker. Bobby suppressed a smile when he noticed that Tommy appeared to be walking a little bit taller and exhibiting a lot more energy.

"Gentlemen," began the president, "before we delve into the terrorist activities in Iraq, I want to take a few minutes to update you on some activities concerning Capitol Hill over the last twenty-four hours. I am sure you are aware of these activities; if not, you will get the media's interpretation here shortly. A little less than twenty-four hours ago, an attempt on my life was thwarted by Bobby and his men. Early this morning, CIA Director Bill Pitts was found dead in his office. While this investigation was ongoing, Senator Stewart Dooley was found dead in his office. He committed suicide by blowing his head off. Right before our gathering, I was informed that Dooley and two accomplices are chief suspects for Pitts's death. Those two accomplices are on the run, but I have good reason to believe they will be in custody by nightfall."

"Were the attempt on your life and the two deaths connected?" asked Duncan.

"We believe that they are, from the information we have gathered thus far," said Patton. "It seems that Dooley attempted to persuade Pitts to partner with him in taking me out. It appears that Pitts declined but then masterminded the assassination attempt and framed Dooley in the process. Of course, Dooley took matters into his own hands. However, he was unaware of the surveillance camera Pitts had on him. When Dooley knew that he would be caught, he committed suicide."

"Those guys were about as dirty as you can get," said General Phillips. "I would rather lick the bottom of my shoes then shake the hand of either one of those guys. Don't expect me to lose any sleep over either one of them."

"I think we all have similar feelings," said Clermont.

There's one more piece to this puzzle," said the President. "It seems that Marty Hickman has gone AWOL."

"What does Hickman have to do with all of this?" asked Duncan.

"We believe Hickman was the mole who has been leaking information. We know he was loyal to Dooley. What we don't know is how much he knew, or whether he was involved in Pitts's murder or the assassination attempt. We hope to find that out real soon. If there are no more questions on this matter, we will get to the business at hand."

The president paused a few moments, but no one said a word. He quickly changed the subject to the hijacking situation.

"I will be going live in a little over an hour," said Patton. "Is everything in place."

"Yes sir," answered General Phillips. "Everything and everyone is ready. There are B-52 and B-2 Spirit bombers on countdown. There are also a few A-10 Thunderbolts, F-15s and F-16s fueling up as we speak, not to mention a few Raptors in the air making sure nothing takes off from Iraq or Iran without a proper welcome. With the exception of the schools and religious structures, Karbala will be annihilated, as you instructed. It will be years, if ever, before that place resembles anything remotely close to a thriving city. There are separate squadrons and intelligence forces monitoring Iran for the slightest hint of military involvement. The monitoring started a couple of hours ago. The Airforce squadrons have been in rotation over Iraq and Iran for the last six hours. The battleships are moving into position as we speak. Baghdad is on radar for a massive strike 24/7, in case you want to take out the country's top brass."

"Excellent," said Patton. "What about Operation Ghost Town?"

"Operation Ghost Town has been activated, and your go-ahead command is the only thing needed. All of the bases are on the ready, and none of the countries where those bases are stationed exhibited any resistance. We have nuclear war heads programmed and ready to hit the major military strongholds of Russia. We also have some SR 71 Blackbirds strategically placed to intercept any warheads Russia may get off."

"I thought the SR 71 was retired years ago."

"Most of them were, sir. A few were kept and maintained for situations like this."

"I know those planes are fast," said Patton, "but can they intercept a missile?"

"Yes, they can," replied Phillips.

"Good job, General," said Patton. "Clermont, what's the latest word from the countries in question?"

"Well," started Clermont, "the Prime Minister did seem a bit upset when he was warned about the strike on Karbala. That city has a lot of religious history for them. He told me he would not stand by and allow the United States to destroy it."

"What did you say?" asked Patton.

"I informed him that his religious structures and schools would not be touched, but I advised him not to be standing anywhere in Karbala for at least a few days. Media outlets in Karbala were also warned of the impending strike and were advised to warn their citizens to either leave the city or seek refuge in the religious structures and schools if they wanted to stay alive. Even after that warning, neither Iraq nor any of the other countries changed their stance."

"Have we heard from Russia?" asked the president?

"Actually, the Russian president himself called and wanted to speak to you. We told him that you were not available. It seems they know we have nuclear warheads pointed in their direction, and he demanded an explanation."

"What did you tell him?"

"First, we asked him why he thought we were pointing nuclear weapons at them? Of course, he wouldn't reveal his sources. Again, the Russian president demanded an explanation. He didn't seem very happy when he was told that was classified information that only you could divulge, and that you would not be available until after the Iraqi hijacking incident was resolved. Then he mumbled something in Russian and instructed me to remind you that Russia had nuclear weapons also."

"What was your response?" asked Patton.

"I just said 'Okie-dokie,' and added that I would tell you."

"John, did you really say that?" asked Duncan?

"I most certainly did. I figured if the world was about to end in the next couple of days, I might as well enjoy it the best I could."

The president and Bobby smiled, while General Phillips and Bryce Duncan shared a good laugh. Tommy released a small chuckle. He was enjoying every minute of this meeting.

"Tommy, you have been pretty quiet. Are there any recent developments you can share with us?" asked Patton.

"As a matter of fact," he said, there are a couple of things you might find encouraging," said Tommy. My source could not talk very long, for obvious reasons, but he was able to communicate two things to me. As far as Iraq backing the terrorist; Mr. President, he said that was true; we're on the right track. My source didn't have time to tell me how to prove it, but was confident we would figure it out. Then he said something that was very interesting. He said the Prime Minister is showing signs of fear and that we should keep the pressure on."

"That I intend to do," said Patton.

"He didn't have time to explain," continued Tommy, "but he emphasized that the United States should stay on the course we're on and keep the pressure on."

"That is reassuring," said Patton. "I wish your source could have told us more."

"So do I. He said he would call me back if he got the chance, but I don't expect that to happen. Mr. President, this is a little off the subject, but do you know that Speaker Graham is leading the impeachment process against you?"

"Yes, the Speaker is just being himself. I expected as much. I have more important things on my plate than to worry about what the Speaker is doing."

"He is also scheduled to be on Michelle Mason's show, which has just started. You know he will attempt to…"

"I know, Tommy, I know," said Patton. "He will attempt to make me look bad; he will attempt to say that I was a bad choice for president. As I said before, Speaker Graham is just being Speaker Graham."

"Speaking of the gentleman from Kentucky," said Bobby, "he's about to appear on Mason's broadcast."

"Turn it on," ordered the president.

Bobby did as he was instructed. After hitting a few buttons, the television screen appeared, tuned to the show.

"Welcome back to coverage of the hijacking of AWA Flight 454. I am Michelle Mason with Channel 8 and we have a lot of information to cover in a little less than an hour. As you may well know, the president of the United States is due to speak live at noon. Our guest speaker this morning is the Speaker of the House, Harry Graham from Kentucky. But before we bring the Speaker out, there is some breaking news that involves government at its highest level."

"CIA Director Bill Pitts's body was found in his office this morning. First appearances indicated that Mr. Pitts had a massive coronary. However, we have since obtained proof that the CIA Director's death was a homicide, and Senator Stewart Dooley might have been directly involved."

"I am told that Pitts' assistant, Ms. Betty Davis Hernandez, gave FBI Director Ray Silva the vital piece of information that led authorities to Senator Dooley. It appears that the CIA director had a glass eye, which was no big secret. However, what Senator Dooley didn't know was that the glass eye contained a video recorder, which not only showed the pictures of Dooley and his accomplices but also captured their self-incriminating words. Senator Dooley's accomplices, John Conklin and Bruce McAllister, are on the run. They are expected to be in custody before night-fall."

"A couple of hours after Pitts's body was found, Senator Dooley's body was found in his office. It seems that the rough-and-tough general committed suicide once he knew he had no way out. The motive for these deaths involves newly elected President Dale Patton. There was no love lost between the president and Senator Dooley, opponents in the recent election. As a matter of fact, that was very evident when I spoke with Senator Dooley yesterday. From what we have gathered, Senator Dooley tried to partner with the CIA director to murder the president. Pitts backed out of the deal, but an attempt was made on the president's life when he went on the air yesterday. Fortunately, that attempt was foiled by the Secret Service. All of the evidence from that assassination attempt pointed to Senator Dooley. Since the inept assassin was a CIA agent, Dooley felt that Pitts set him up and took matters into his own hands. Thus, we have two deaths and three people on the run."

"The third person of interest is Secret Service Agent Marty Hickman. Agent Hickman was a friend to Senator Dooley and a possible third accomplice. He is also believed to be the White House mole who has been leaking information. Needless to say, the president has extra security around him at all times, at least until all of the loose ends have been tied up."

"As I told you earlier, a lot has been going on in the area. It looks as if the new president is up to his ears in murder, betrayal, and terrorism. However, that's not the only thing President Patton is facing in his first three days on the job. I have to take a station break, but don't go anywhere. I'll be back in two minutes to tell you all about the latest rumor."

"What else am I going through, Tommy?" Patton asked with a big smile."

"Well, sir," he replied, she will probably bring up the impeachment process, being spear-headed by Senator Graham."

"Of course," said Patton. "As a matter of fact, I have a meeting with the goon squad later today to discuss my impeachment."

"She will probably try to get a few ratings points by bringing up how all of this has affected your marriage."
Before the President could reply, Katie walked in, to everyone's surprise. Even Bobby was caught off guard, if that was possible. Everyone instantly stood up to welcome the first lady. Katie walked straight to her husband and gave him a big hug and a kiss.

"I think our marriage is just fine," said Katie, "so that should be a heart-warming, feel-good kind of story. What do you think, Dale?"
Everyone started to clap. Katie was back to her old self. Dale was all smiles and couldn't help but to stare lovingly at his wife. He was feeling so alive and so confident right about now.

"I'm confused," he said. "Was there ever a problem with our marriage?"

"You're sweet," said Katie, "but you guys need to get back to work. The program is coming back on, and I know you want to hear what the Speaker has to say."

"We all know what he's going to say. There won't be any surprises in that respect," said Patton.

"Don't worry," she said, "I'll be around. I'm not going anywhere. Now go get those bastards."

Katie kissed her husband on the cheek, turned and left the room. The president watched her for a few seconds. He didn't know what had brought her around, but he was glad she was back. He didn't care what happened now. He felt as if he could take on the world. The show was coming back on. Patton returned to his seat and gave the screen his full attention.

"This is Michelle Mason once again, reporting on the hijacking of AWA Flight 454. Newly elected President Dale Patton will address the situation in about forty-five minutes. Before he comes on, let me continue where I left off. As I was saying, not only is the president battling murder, betrayal, and terrorism, but rumor has it that all of this is putting a strain on his marriage. As a matter of fact, it's being said that the first lady is holding the president personally responsible for the death of her mother, and she is contemplating a divorce."

"I think that's referred to as sensationalism, negligent reporting, and a bold face lie, all rolled up into one," Katie aid from off-camera. Mason looked over in the direction of the voice. You could have knocked her over with a feather when she saw the first lady standing in the wings. This was not scripted, and she did not have an automatic comeback line.

"Uh, Mrs. Patton, I didn't know you were here. I wasn't expecting you. Come on out."

"I think it's petty evident that you weren't expecting me. I gave you more credit than being a gossip-spreading journalist."

"Are you implying there is no truth to the information I just shared with our viewers?" Mason asked.

"No," said Katie, "I am not implying anything. I am saying outright there is no truth to it. You could have at least talked to me before you reported on rumors."

"With all due respect, Mrs. Patton, my sources are, and have always been, top notch. I have never reported anything that wasn't the absolute truth. Could it be you're trying to mask the truth to protect the affairs of the White House?"

"With all due respect, Ms. Mason, the information you shared with your viewers about my husband and I, are not true, and I invite you to prove me wrong. Furthermore, by suggesting I don't want the truth told to protect something or someone, implies that I am lying. I resent being called a liar. As you just reported, the White House has an information leak; over the last few days, you have reported confidential information which was not officially shared with you. I would double-check my sources if I were you. If your sources and the leak are one in the same, you could find yourself in a very uncomfortable conversation with the FBI. I wish I could stay longer, but I had planned to watch my husband's response in another location."

Katie got up and walked off the set. Michelle Mason was in an uncomfortable and unfamiliar situation. This was the second time that the first lady had made her look like an amateur. Not only did she put a big dent in her credibility, but she also threatened a federal investigation on a criminal offense.

The problem was that Katie was correct. Though it had only been a few seconds, it seemed like fifteen minutes with the cameras still rolling. The first lady had taken the punches of the hard-hitting journalist and floored her with an unseen counterpunch. Michelle Mason immediately went to a commercial break.

"Damn," said Duncan, "all of the Pattons play rough, don't they? I have never seen anyone back Michelle down like that."

"That wasn't rough," said Patton. "Katie took it easy on her because she was on camera."

"She has impeccable timing," said Tommy. "That was how she was when she showed up at the original press conference a couple of days ago. Just like then, she got the media off our back. With all due respect, Mr. President, the first lady has been an asset."

"Tommy, stay away from my wife's assets," said Patton. "Bobby, keep your eye on Tommy."

"You got it, boss," Bobby said, smiling.

"Alright, everybody quiet down," ordered Patton, "the broadcast is coming back on."

Patton and Bobby's dialog got a few chuckles from everybody. It was all in fun, and Tommy knew it. He had to smile himself. He was in; he was one of the boys. Tommy thought it an honor that the President had teased him in front of everyone. It took all he had to stay focused on the screen.

Michelle Mason had regained most of her composure. She watched the countdown to return to the airwaves for her live telecast. She had been deep in thought during the commercial break. She had never thought twice about the source of her informants until Katie mentioned it. She knew it was probably an internal leak from the White House, but this wasn't the first time. Someone was always leaking information from the White House trying to gain power by squealing on, discrediting, or embarrassing a colleague. However, it had never ended in murder or suicide.

"Hello ladies and gentlemen, and welcome back. Our next guest is none other than the Speaker of the House, Senator Harry Graham, from Kentucky. Speaker Graham's assessment of the way the newly elected President is handling the hostage situation is similar to those of the late Senator Dooley. As you remember, Senator Dooley was my guest on yesterday's show. Who knew that less than twenty-four hours later he would be dead? I want to thank you, Mr. Speaker, for agreeing to appear on such short notice."

"It is my pleasure, Ms. Mason."

"Mr. Speaker, what is wrong with the way the President is handling this terrorist situation?"

"The President is out of control," said Graham. "He is making this personal. He is using the fine men and women of our military for his personal agenda. Dooley was correct; he's out of control."

"Mr. Speaker, rumor has it that you're leading the charge to have the president removed from office. Is that true?"

"If the President continues on the course he's on, he will remove himself from office. I am just one of many who has recognized this and who is determined not to let him act like some cocky teenager whose testosterone is in overdrive."

"But sir, this is only the president's third day in office."

"How long do you suggest we give him to put us in the middle of a war? Ms. Mason, the president is about to attack a country with no evidence of their involvement in the killing of our citizens. He has completely by-passed protocol and has ignored Congress. He's a career soldier who is doing what he does best. He thinks everything can be solved with his fist or a gun."

"He is the commander-in-chief," Mason said, "and has the authority to act as such when our country has been threatened."

"Ms. Mason, allow me to repeat myself. There is no evidence of any country's involvement in the hijacking of AWA Flight 454. Dale Patton is on course to serve the shortest presidential term in US history and maybe some prison time."

"The American people disagree with you."

"I suppose you're about to give me the results of some biased popularity poll."

"Sort of, but it's more than a popularity poll. It started out that way, but it looks as if it's growing into a movement."

"Most movements are short lived," said Graham, "just like this president's time in office."

"Well, Mr. Speaker, it seems that the American people approve of the way the President is handling the hijacking situation. Our station was going to survey the handling of the hijacking situation, but we discovered that it is being widely discussed among the major social networks. Facebook users are starting a serious movement and have already collected two and a half million signatures. All this has happened in the last two days."

"Signatures are good, but they won't keep the president in office."

"Maybe not," she said, "but over three hundred and fifty thousand of those signatures are from your home state of Kentucky. It appears that you, Speaker Graham, have been identified as the main antagonist against the president. Those signatures are from registered voters who have pledged to vote against you in the upcoming election in May. A large percentage of those Kentucky signatures have said that you will not run unopposed in the primary. They will find a challenger and vote against you. You see, Mr. Speaker, the reason behind those signatures is to remove you from office."

Harry Graham was visibly upset. His face turned red as he loosened his tie. This had blindsided him; he was not prepared to address his re-election.

"I doubt if there is much for me to be concerned about," said Graham. "I would have been informed if this little social network movement was a threat to me."

"Maybe you've been so busy trying to remove the new president that you overlooked the trouble brewing in your own backyard," Mason said. This little social network movement, as you call it, is keeping the county clerk offices in Kentucky very busy. It seems that statewide more than fifty thousand registration cards have been requested from voters wanting to change their party affiliation; to be able to vote against you. Slightly more than ten thousand people statewide have already switched from republican to democrat, just in case you win the primary. This is going on all over the country, but it seems that Kentucky is leading the way. It seems that this little social network movement is pretty powerful and is starting to snowball."

The Speaker cleared his throat as beads of sweat became noticeable on his forehead. He squinted and looked at Mason as if he wanted to strangle her. She added a little more fuel to the flame.

"You know, Mr. Speaker, if you and a few more republicans do not survive this year's election in your home states, the president will have a Democratic Congress and the Speaker of the House will be a Democrat."

"Ms. Mason," began the Speaker, "your very transparent attempt to try and protect President Patton will not work. First, I believe you have blown this social network story out of proportion, either to try and scare me or to try and give the country a hint of what you would like to see. Whether your story is true or not, the president has acted irrationally and beyond his authority. Therefore, he must be held responsible for his actions."

"With all due respect, Mr. Speaker," countered Mason, "I don't create the news, I report it. All you have to do is make a phone call. I am sure no clerk office in Kentucky is too busy to take a call from its home-grown Speaker of the House."

"It's been interesting, Ms. Mason, but I have work to do and must be going. A few of us will be meeting with the president later today to put him on notice. Maybe Channel 8 will consider an out-of-work President for employment."

Harry Graham removed his microphone, placed it in his seat, and walked off the set. The cameras followed him until he disappeared behind the curtain. Mason also followed the Senator's departure, all the time fighting back a smile.

"Well, we can't seem to keep any of our guests on the set today. Actually, that was very timely because the president is ready to address those responsible for the hijacking of AWA Flight 454. We will break for a few minutes, and then our station manager will be back to introduce President Dale Patton."

Bobby and the security detail waited to escort the president to the set. Patton made one last check to make sure everything and everyone was ready. General Phillips and Bryce Duncan had assured him all branches of the military were not only ready, but anxious to get started. Patton checked in one last time with Darrin by phone.

"I'm close, boss," said Darrin. "Tommy called me with a lead that looks as if it might pay off."

"I hope so," replied Patton. "I am going to need that proof sooner than planned after I give my response tonight."

"Dale, what are you going to do?"

"You'll know in a few minutes. Just get me that proof. I'm counting on you, Darrin."

"I'm on it. I feel really good about this. Just don't take any unnecessary risks. Senator Graham and a few others are already out to hang you. Don't give them anymore rope. "

"I'll try to remember that. I have to go on live television. Get me that proof!"

Patton ended the connection and gave the phone to Tommy, who placed it back on the base. Patton headed to the set, surrounded by the Secret Service, with Bobby leading the way. Tommy, Bryce, and General Phillips focused their attention back on the large-screen television to watch the president's response. General Phillips picked up the remote to the television and pressed a button. The television screen split into a double screen. On the left was Channel 8, in which the President would soon be on. On the right was a station that could only be reached by a special satellite. It was focused in on Karbala, which would be in ruins in less than thirty minutes.

"Welcome back; this is a Channel 8 special broadcast," said Sam Garrett with a cordless microphone in hand. "In just a few moments, we will be live with the president of the United States. As he makes his way to the set, let me update you on the latest news of the hijacking of AWA Flight 454. It is my understanding that another tape was sent to the President. Channel 8 was not able to get a copy of that tape. However, we have been told that it showed the terrorists killing more of the hostages. The big news is that the president's mother-in-law was one of the people supposedly killed. Katie Patton's mother, Katherine Morrison, was brutally murdered, and a tape of it was sent to the president. We are anxious to hear what the president will say today in response to this heinous act. I see that the president has now arrived and is ready to take the stage. Without further delay America, I introduce the President of the United States, Dale Patton."

The president and Sam Garrett walked toward each other. They briefly shook hands as the president positioned himself at the podium and Garrett walked off stage. Bobby, Keith, and another one of Bobby's men took their places alongside each camera. They didn't expect another assassination attempt, but they weren't taking any chances. The president appeared relaxed and confident. Again, he was using no Teleprompters.

"Ladies and gentlemen, once again I appear before you to address an evil that is inflicting pain and death on some of our citizens. However, before I address that evil, I would first like to address the American people. I would like to thank you for your support. I am aware of some of the things going on in support of the way that I am handing the hijacking situation, and I want to thank you for it. It gives me great gratitude and peace of mind to know that the American people approve of the decisions that I am making. Our country is like a small, close knit community; when one of us hurt, we all hurt, and when a bully attacks one of us, he must deal with all of us. We are one big family, and nothing or no one, not even elected officials, should prevent us from protecting our family. Elected officials can be removed from office, but some of you are well aware of this, because such a process has already begun in Kentucky. I applaud you for being proactive instead of reactive."

"Now, to address the situation for which I am here. I have only a few things to say. Iraq, you have responded to my first appearance by taking more innocent lives. That cannot, and will not be ignored. In a matter of hours, Karbala will cease to exist. With the exception of its schools and its historic and religious structures, that city will be rubble. The United States will lead a strike against Karbala in retaliation for Iraq's blatant torture and murder of our citizens. Your remaining forty-eight hours have been cut in half. You now only have twenty-four hours, at most, to release our citizens. I say 'at most' because Iraq will be instantly attacked without warning, and without mercy, if there is additional torture or murder of any of the passengers from AWA Flight 454. As bad as Karbala will look in a few hours, it will look like a paradise compared to the rest of Iraq if anyone else from that plane is injured. Iraq, you have been warned."

The President left the podium and walked off the set. He was instantly surrounded by Secret Service Agents, led by Bobby. They headed back to the war room. Sam Garrett reappeared in front of the cameras, still holding the cordless microphone.

"Ladies and gentlemen, we have to go to a commercial break. But, we will be back to wrap up this telecast with a few remarks regarding the president's very short response."

CHAPTER TWENTY-TWO

The president and Bobby entered the war room as some of the security detail took their places outside the door, while the others secured the floor. Tommy and General Phillips were glued to the television. Bryce Duncan and John Clermont were busy on the phone and trying to watch the fall of Karbala at the same time. The president took his seat, and Bobby returned to his station directly behind him. The television had been switched back to a single screen and tuned in to the satellite feed. They watched as bombers began attacking Karbala.

The cover of night was soon lifted as Karbala began to glow. It was not the gentle, inviting glow of a sunrise, but the flickering, burning brightness of a live blaze. The city was on fire. Bombs fell like rain as structure after structure disintegrated. The bombers made a couple of passes and hit targets with uncanny accuracy. As they were making their first pass, they were confronted by a squadron of Iranian fighters. They came from the east as the bombers were approaching from the south. The lead plane had the B-52 in its cross hairs and was about to take the kill shot. Before the pilot could pull the trigger, a missile pierced the night air and turned the Iranian fighter into a fireworks display. Without warning, the four other fighters were destroyed in the same manner. Seconds later, a squadron of F-16s slowly descended from the clouds.

"Impressive," said President Patton, "very impressive."

"Thank you, sir," said General Phillips. "Those guys are the best of the best. They were thrilled with your decision to go after Iraq."

"I hope they're not trigger happy," replied the president.

"Maybe just a little, Mr. President, but they signed up to protect the country, and what better way to do that than to fight to free innocent American citizens at the mercy of a hostile government?"

"I agree," said the President.

The bombers continued on their run. Their escorts stayed with them for a few minutes, but there were no more attacks. The squadron of F-16s flew back up into the clouds. Downed power lines and broken gas lines caused explosions throughout Karbala. Power plants and water reservoirs were destroyed. Some of the fires were snuffed by flooding, but there were other scenes of fire floating down the street. The bombers were about finished. It was time for the fighters to make their run.

Two squadrons dropped from the sky. The F-15 and F-16 fighters flew over Karbala and surgically removed everything of significance that the bombs didn't finish off. Grocery stores, car lots, small buildings, malls, and movie theatres were all destroyed. The precision of the pilots was amazing. No target was shot at twice. As Patton had instructed, only the schools and religious structures were spared. Not one living creature was seen on the streets, not even pets. Apparently the advanced warning had been taken seriously, and adhered to.

The destruction of Karbala was complete. The once vibrant, beautiful city now resembled a war zone. Very few streets extended further than two blocks without being interrupted by destruction. There was no sign of life beyond the structures that were spared. Even the schools and religious structures were dark, with the exception of a few flickering candles and oil lamps. As much as despair and hopelessness were represented by the isolated fires, they also resembled hope, faith, and mercy. The majority of the schools and religious structures appeared to be located in the center of the city. The fires circled around these structures as if to highlight and showcase them; as if to say, 'You have been spared for a reason.' Plumes of smoke began to rise skyward as if to be waving a big white flag. It was a very powerful visual.

"Did you imagine this picture, Mr. President," asked Clermont, "when you decided to spare those structures?"

"No, I didn't, but I'm glad it turned out this way. Karbala has a lot of religious history and culture, and I wanted to preserve that. I figured that would be something for them to look to and to build on."

"And if more hostages are killed?" asked General Phillips.

"You heard my response on live television," said Patton. "I wasn't bluffing."

"Speaking of response," said Duncan, "it appears that there was very little resistance to our strike."

"I concur," said Clermont, "very little resistance but a lot of veiled threats and political finger-pointing."

"That one Iranian squadron was the only resistance?"

"Yes sir," said General Phillips, "that was it, and I don't expect anything else. Iraq's military had already been incapacitated, and we didn't expect anything from them. We did think Iran would offer more resistance, but they probably changed their minds when they saw how easily and effortlessly their fighters were destroyed."

"What about Russia?" asked the president.

"Good question. We haven't heard a peep from Russia. Of course, our entire military is on guard 24/7 until this situation has been resolved. We are not dismissing anyone, no matter how much or little we have heard from them."

"I think Russia is looking for an out," said Clermont, "and you were wise enough to give them one. Iraq is the only one under the spotlight. They were the only country pressured to make a decision under the eyes of the entire world. By not bringing attention to any of the other countries that threatened us, no one knows of their involvement. They can always deny any accusation we make by simply not getting involved. Iran might have a hard time explaining the loss of five planes, but it can be done."

"Regardless, all systems, including Ghost Town, remain active until I cancel them. Good work from each of you. Stay on top of this situation. I want to know if there are any civilian or military casualties. John, I want to be notified immediately if Iraq contacts us."

"You can bank on it, sir," replied Clermont.

"Well, gentlemen, we have reached a point of no return. To be more accurate, I have reached a point of no return. You were just following orders. By my command, the United States has used military force against another country without proof of the charges for which I have accused them. True, I did not have the approval of Congress or the UN, and concrete proof would have guaranteed their cooperation. Senator Graham may be correct; I may serve the shortest term of any US president."

"I doubt if that will be the case," said Tommy. "Darrin is working on that proof as we speak, and he is pretty confident he has something."

"If anyone can find it, Darrin can. I'm not throwing in the towel, just stating the facts. As a matter of fact, I am betting that the start of my second term won't top this."

"Hopefully, we won't have to deal with Harry Graham during your second term," said Tommy. "I hear things are not looking too promising for him being re-elected."

"I hope you're right, but I could be gone by May myself. I am sure in our meeting later today he will inform me of their intentions to start the impeachment process."

"I am sure you're correct, Mr. President," said Clermont, "but an impeachment proceeding can be dragged out for months. Sir, you know as well as I that the success of this situation, or lack thereof, will play a huge part on how successful the impeachment process will be. It will determine if there will even be an impeachment hearing."

"You're absolutely right, John, but the return of the majority of the hostages is the only way this situation can even remotely be considered somewhat of a success. That is looking less likely with every passing minute."

"Speaking of hostages," said Duncan, "it appears that Ockbar Shalam is the one we should be talking to about returning our citizens.

There is a slight possibility that we could be wrong about Iraq's involvement."

"Wouldn't that be a nail in my coffin?" said the President.

"I hope that didn't come across as a personal desire. I was simply making sure that all bases were covered."

Patton gave Duncan an intense stare for a couple of seconds. He didn't believe for a minute that Duncan was hoping for his demise, but he did want him to know he still had a few doubts about him.

"Iraq may not be involved," said the president, "but I don't believe that for a second. Even if I am wrong, we are in too deep, and too many innocent people have died to change course now. We have to play out our hand. The prime minister loves that country. Even if Iraq is not involved, I am betting he will do anything to prevent more devastation. He knows he does not have the firepower to challenge us. His only recourse is to help us out....if he can."

"Well," began Tommy, "as I mentioned earlier, my sources say the prime minister is fit to be tied. If that is true, and I believe it is, he is probably panicking right about now after the destruction of Karbala and having only twenty-four hours to release the hostages."

"That's all well and good," said Duncan, "but Ockbar has the hostages, and he is hundreds of miles away from the prime minister. As far as we know that maniac could be filming another execution as we speak."

"I pray that's not the case," said Patton, "for Iraq's sake."

All eyes were on the president. Was he serious? He had just threatened to destroy Iraq if the hostages were not released in less than twenty-four hours. He said this with the entire world watching and without concrete proof that Iraq was directly involved. Congress would have no choice but to impeach him. He would be extremely fortunate if impeachment was the only action that was brought against him. He would probably be charged with murder and several other national and international crimes.

"You can't be serious," said Duncan. "You would be cutting your own throat."

"I didn't know you cared Bryce," said Patton. "I'm deeply touched, but I never bluff."

"This is the second time that I have heard you say that you never bluff. Now I understand," said Tommy.

"What do you understand?" asked Patton.

"I understand why Bobby called you a lousy poker player. I thought you guys were trying to bait me, but you were serious."

All eyes turned to Tommy. They couldn't believe he was talking about poker. They were all concerned with impeachment proceedings, murder charges, mass destruction, and a possible world war, and Tommy was talking about poker. Where was this guy from? they thought. Tommy knew exactly what they were thinking. He could read their eyes as if they were speaking out loud.

"Either you're in or you're out," said Tommy. "We're in too deep to think about consequences at this point. The president told you his stance, and I'm pretty sure he's not going to change his mind. All of this disbelief and criticism is counterproductive and distracting. You look at me like I'm from another planet, but you act like sissies with your trousers around your ankles. Through this whole ordeal, the president has done exactly what he said he would do, so this shouldn't be so shocking to you."

Bobby and the president caught each other's eye. They didn't expect this from Tommy, but they were glad to see it. Tommy was proving to be more of an asset and more loyal than the president ever thought he would be. Maybe Tommy should be his chief of staff.

"I don't know about the rest of these guys," said Tommy, "but I'm still with you. What's our next move, sir?"

"Well, first I think the guys need to pull their trousers up," said the president. "We just wait for now. The next move is up to Iraq."

Bobby and Tommy couldn't help letting out a little chuckle. Duncan, Clermont, and General Phillips hung their heads. They were angry, embarrassed, and humiliated all at the same time. They would not underestimate Tommy again.

CHAPTER TWENTY-THREE

"Iraq, you have been warned," said President Patton, as Ockbar again studied the body language of the American President. The terrorist was getting angrier by the minute. He had been totally ignored. At least during his first response, the US President had referred to him as a joker. This time, he was treated as if he didn't exist; even worse, he was treated as if he didn't matter. This was driving Ockbar crazy. He was the mastermind behind all of this; he was the one who deserved the credit.

Ockbar turned the television off. He did not want to hear anything else from the president. It was right at that moment that Ockbar heard and felt the thunder of the bombs dropping close by. He went outside and looked to his north. The sky was lit up like the aurora borealis. President Patton was bombing Karbala. He didn't consider Ockbar enough of a concern to bomb, or even shoot a few rounds in his direction; he didn't even try to scare him.

Ockbar knew his next production had to be big; big enough to get the president's undivided attention. A wicked smile came across Ockbar's face. Just as he was getting an idea of what he would do, his phone rang. Ockbar removed his phone from his pocket and answered it after quickly glancing at the digital display.

"Everything is under control, Mr. Prime Minister," said Ockbar, "but I may need some additional assistance."

"How can you say everything is under control when Karbala is being turned into a wasteland? The American President knows of our involvement. How did that happen? You were supposed to keep the country out of this. You promised me," said the Prime Minister.

"The American President knows nothing," replied Ockbar, "he is bluffing."

"Those are not bluffs raining down on Karbala. The United States does not threaten war on a bluff," said the prime minister. "True, they are a country full of talkers and negotiators, but they only strike after months of collecting information or after they have undeniable proof that warrants a strike. The Americans must know something for them to strike so quickly."

"I repeat, everything is under control," said an irritated Ockbar. "The United States does not know of Iraq's involvement. I need your help to make a statement on US soil. Are you going to help me finish this or not?"

"You are an imbecile, and you're in over your head," said the prime minister right before he ended the call.

"Hello, hello," repeated Ockbar," and then he put his phone back in his pocket. "I will teach you to hang up on me. I will take care of you as soon as I destroy the American president. You're a coward. "This is not the business for cowards."

Ockbar walked back into the building, looking for Rahman. He was ready to start planning his next production. This would be something the world would not forget.

"Rahman, come here," said Ockbar as he walked toward him.

"You looked pissed off," said Rahman. "What's wrong?"

"The American president has the prime minister wetting his pants, and he's trying to put pressure on me. Have Abdul and the others ready to film in a few hours. I'm going to send the American president a production he will never forget."

"What do you have in mind?"

"My next production will have child stars. There are at least four or five kids on board aren't there?"

"Yes," said Rahman, "but are you sure you want to do this?"

"Why wouldn't I? I am prepared to do whatever has to be done. I want to see how tall the American president stands and how confident he sounds when children start to die."

"I don't think the American president will back down. You are two of a kind. Again, I say you have underestimated this man."

"So, you think we should tuck our tails between our legs and run. Is that it, Rahman?"

"No, that is not what I said. We need to find another way. Killing children is not the answer. Killing children should be our trump card when all else fails. You sound desperate Ockbar."

"I am not desperate, I am angry, and I think it is the answer. You forget we have another trump card if this fails. Either you're with me or you're against me. Which one is it?"

"Don't test me, Ockbar. I told you once before that I don't fear any man, and that includes you. I am not one of your mindless minions. I follow because I choose to. You know I am with you. I just don't like killing children."

"Noted, now let's get to work. Take some children from the plane and put them in the workshop. I want all of the children less than ten years of age if they are available. If not, get what you can, but no babies, not yet anyway. I want them to stay in the workshop for a couple of hours so that the fear will be fresh on their faces when it's time to film."

"As you wish," said Rahman as he walked away, "but that so-called trump card you mentioned has been played once. It didn't work then, and it won't work later."

Rahman left the building and headed for the hangar. He was against harming children, but he would do as Ockbar had asked this time. Rahman had already determined that Ockbar was letting his ego get in the way and was not thinking clearly. The American President was as stubborn as Ockbar and would not bulge. Killing the children could work, but Rahman doubted it. Besides, this was his trump card. If this did not work, Ockbar had nothing else to threaten the President with. Rahman concluded that if this did not work, he may have to retire

Ockbar and take over the operation. The two of them had worked together many times, but Ockbar was letting personal issues interfere with business.

Rahman opened the door of the hangar and walked toward the plane. He looked around in an attempt to find Abdul. He saw him and a couple of the other terrorists talking near the steps of the plane. They appeared to be in a spirited discussion.

"Abdul," shouted Rahman, "come over here."

Abdul turned to see who was calling him. He slowly walked over to Rahman.

"What is going on over there," asked Rahman? "You guys seem to be disagreeing about something. Is everything okay?"

"Yes, everything is fine. I just don't like the way those bastards talk down at us sometimes. They think they are better than us because they work for Saheed el-Ali. When this is over, I will show them who is better."

"Forget about them, Abdul. The prime minister is probably chewing their ass like he is trying to chew Ockbar's. El-Ali is not happy with the way things are going, and he may have cut us off. Keep your eyes and ears open."

"Just say the word; I'm just waiting for a reason to slaughter some pigs."

"Listen up, Abdul; Ockbar wants us to be ready to shoot another production in a few hours. He wants to take four or five kids from the plane and make them the star of the next shoot."

"You can't be serious," said Abdul. "When did we start killing kids?"

"I know. I feel the same way. I tried to talk him out of it, but he tried to turn it around and make me seem soft. I will do it this time, but if it doesn't work, he better watch his back. Are you with me?"

"Yeah, I'm with you, Rahman. You and I worked together before Ockbar came on the scene. You should be running this operation anyway."

"Come on, let's go grab some kids off the plane and get the camera equipment ready," Rahman said as they walked toward the steps of the plane.

Ruth Wilcox was growing extremely agitated. She looked as if she was on the verge of a nervous breakdown. She had managed to settle down enough to control her trembling episodes, but she was still sweating profusely. Why was Katherine so stubborn? Why didn't she listen to reason? All she had to do was sit still and keep her mouth shut, but she couldn't do that. They were such opposites that Ruth couldn't recall how they came to be such good friends, but she loved the woman dearly.

Tears rolled down Ruth's cheeks; she couldn't take her eyes off of her battered and beaten friend. She adjusted Katherine's pillow to try and make her more comfortable, but she was too bruised and battered to relax. Katherine was grateful that she had been returned to the plane, but Ruth's sniffles and constant pampering began to wear on her nerves.

"Get a grip, Ruth," said Katherine. "I'm a little sore and bruised, but I'm alright. You sound worse than I look. Calm down and try to get some rest. Who knows what else is in store for us?"

"Katherine, you're so, so mangled. How can you be so calm?"

"What choice do I have?"

"Aren't you afraid that they're not finished with you? You're still connected to the president. They may come back and pick up where they left off."

"I'm sure of it," said Katherine. "There's not a doubt in my mind that they're not finished with me. I was afraid at first, but not anymore. Believe it or not, I am at peace."

At that moment, everyone's attention turned toward the door of the plane. They could hear voices right outside the door, and then they heard the handle rattle as it did when someone was entering. As the door slowly opened, the air inside the plane seemed to have been sucked out. Breathing became difficult for the hostages, and a few of them began to hyperventilate. Eyes and ears strained to identify the evil that was now present. Although terrorists remained on the plane around the clock, they were different. They were obedient hounds who rarely caused a problem without a command from their master. The door of the plane was feared. The door seemed to always allow death to enter. The question was who had death come to claim? This was the fear that occupied the thoughts of each hostage.

Rahman and Abdul entered and walked a few steps up the aisle. Rahman glanced around as if he was looking for someone. He then began to count out loud. A very observant woman spoke up before she realized her lips had betrayed her thoughts.

"He's counting the children," she said, horrified. "They're going to kill the children."

Screams and sobs could be heard throughout the plane. Parents grabbed their children and hugged them tight. All the hostages had tears in their eyes, including the men.

Katherine began to stand up, but Ruth held her down.

"What do you think you're doing? Haven't you been beat enough? You're asking for a death sentence. Do you want to die?"

"I am already dead," said Katherine. "That's why I am at peace."

"What are you talking about?"

"When they had me out there in front of the camera, they killed me."

"You have been beaten too badly; you're hallucinating. Sit back and pray that they leave us alone."

"I can't do that," said Katherine. "There are children's lives at stake. Ruth, they killed me to the world. I have nothing else to lose."

"What are you saying? I don't understand."

"When they had me in front of the camera, I saw the red light go off right before they fired the pistol. That was more than just a scare tactic. They killed everyone else out there except me. They left me alive for one reason, and that is to keep using me as the main hostage. They want my daughter and the rest of the world to think I am dead. Then they will put me in front of the camera again and make more demands. These people play off of our fear and emotions. I know Dale won't budge, but I am not sure what kind of emotional roller coaster that would be for Katie. I think they are going to kill me eventually anyway. Maybe I can do some good before I go."

Ruth did not know what to say. She had not thought about why they had let Katherine live. She was just glad she was alive. Unfortunately, it all made sense. Ruth knew she was right. She could feel her grip loosen on her arm as she gathered herself to stand.

Although Rahman had counted seven children who he thought would be appropriate, he would only take five. He believed that they were between the ages of three and ten years old. Each child would cry every time Rahman looked in his or her general direction, and the parent would pull the child in close. Rahman said something in his native tongue, and the four terrorists who had already been standing guard on the plane paid close attention to him.

Rahman pointed at a little boy who appeared to be about six. One of the terrorists walked toward him and pulled him from his father's arms. As the boy was pulled up the aisle, the father started after them, but then froze in his tracks. The terrorist had pulled his pistol and pointed it at him.

"That's my son, my only son!" he shouted, with tears streaming down his face.

"Go back to your seat or your only son will watch his father die."

"I will trade my life for my son's any day."

"Who mentioned anything about a trade," asked the gunman?

The father began to slowly walk toward the gunman. A collective gasp filled the air. Faint sobs and sniffles were heard throughout the plane. A few people cupped their hands over their mouth and nose in a praying motion. The little boy was reaching out for his father as his father inched closer.

"I will die before I let you take my son."

The gunman lowered his pistol and squeezed off a round, hitting the father in his left thigh. Blood squirted in the air, and the father fell to the floor. He clutched his leg as the blood flowed out: he grimaced as he applied pressure to his leg in an attempt to stop the bleeding.

"I want you to witness what's in store for your son," said the gunman. "You can die later."

A couple of passengers helped the father back to his seat. One removed his belt and fastened it round his leg to create a tourniquet. The father was ready to get back up but his fellow passengers kept him in his seat.

Rahman pointed at a little girl who appeared to be about the same age as the boy. The boy was handed over to Abdul and the gunman went after the little girl. Her mother was hysterical. She cried and held on to her daughter as the gunman slowly approached. People began to pray out loud. The name of Jesus filled the air and "God help us" could be heard often.

The gunman stopped at the girl and began to pull her from her mother's arms. The woman fought furiously to keep her child. The gunman took a step back and pointed his pistol at the woman's head.

"We can do this the easy way or an even easier way," said the gunman.

Katherine had made it to her feet and shouted at the gunman, "The children are innocent. Leave them alone."

The gunman turned his head in Katherine's direction and pointed his pistol at her. Rahman looked on without interfering. He was interested in this confrontation. They had orders not to harm Katherine, but Rahman figured she had served her purpose.

"Go back to your seat, or your journey ends here and now."

"Your owner did not give you permission to speak," said Katherine. "Now be a good doggie and lick the little girl's hand and then go somewhere and lick yourself."

The gunman turned and walked toward Katherine. She stood her ground as he approached. Ruth was crying uncontrollably, as were many others. She knew nothing good could come from this. The gunman's jaws tightened, and he clenched his teeth. The scowl on his face was proof that Katherine's comment had hit a nerve. He looked down on her as if she was horse manure on the bottom of his shoe.

WILLIAM I. BRAZLEY JR.

"Your mouth is going to be the death of you sooner than planned," said the gunman.

"Why don't you take me and leave the kids alone? It's obvious you want to hurt me, so why not take me up on my offer?"

"You're right, I do want to hurt you, but you're not in a position to bargain. Why should I choose between the two when I can hurt you and the children?"

With that said, the gunman swung his pistol and struck the left side of Katherine's face. She was not able to break her fall, because she was out cold before she hit the floor. Her left cheekbone looked fractured, as blood oozed from her ear. Ruth jumped to her aid. She dabbed at the blood with the handkerchief she had been crying into. Ruth cried and flailed her arms and cried some more as she called out to Katherine.

The gunman walked back toward the little girl. As he did, a couple of men picked Katherine up and placed her back in her seat. Ruth reached over and tilted Katherine's seat back and tried to make her comfortable. Ruth convinced herself that her friend was resting. Yes, she would be in a lot of pain when she woke up, but at least she was resting at the moment. Ruth would soon come to realize that Katherine was dead.

"Get on with it," said Rahman. "You're wasting time."

The gunman cocked his hand back as if he was going to strike the woman in the same manner as he did Katherine. When she covered her face with one arm, the gunman yanked the little girl from her mother's grasp. The mother attempted to get up, but was shoved back into her seat. She looked up to see the barrel of the pistol pointed at her. The young mother cried and screamed as she watched her sobbing child being taken away.

This scene continued three more times. Two more little boys and another little girl were snatched from their parent's grasp. On each occasion, the parent was threatened or beaten or both to force them to relinquish their child. A woman, who would not stop fighting for her child, was shot in the leg in the same manner as the first parent.

She too was carried back to her seat and cared for by some concerned passengers.

Rahman, Abdul, and another terrorist corralled the children as the gunman rounded up the children that Rahman pointed out. The mood on the plane went up and down like a roller coaster ride. One minute the cabin would be deathly quiet, with every parent praying that his or her child would not be selected. The next minute screams, crying, and prayers filled the cabin. Parents were crying for their children; children were crying for their parents; and rows and rows of scared passengers were crying for both.

Rahman and Abdul kept the children that had been selected in the front of the plane for a couple of minutes, in full view of everyone. The other four terrorist kept everyone in their seats with threats of violence. The fear index went through the roof, and Rahman soaked in every second of it as if he was being fed. After finally getting their fill, Rahman and Abdul led the children off the plane and slammed the door behind them.

The children slowly descended the steps. Abdul tried to hurry them, but their little water-filled eyes made the steps difficult to maneuver. When they reached the bottom, they were marched out the hangar and into the smaller building. The children were taken straight to the workshop. Rahman opened the door, and Abdul shoved them inside. All five children began to cry extremely hard. Rahman could not take it. He hurried away out of earshot. The children's eyes had not adjusted yet, so they could not see anything. They stood in the middle of the floor and wailed until they were too exhausted to stand. Although they did not know each other, they felt more comfortable amongst each other. They slumped to the floor as a group and eventually fell asleep in the dark.

"It is as you instructed," said Rahman. "Five children have been secured and await your next production"

"Excellent," replied Ockbar. "I know you don't agree, Rahman, but trust me on this. The American president will regret not giving me the credit I deserve."

"You and the American president are two of a kind. Neither of you know when to back off."

"Back off? You mean give up, don't you? I will never give up to the American dogs."

Abdul had made his way back into the hangar. He had a few more words for the prime minister's men. He did not care if they worked for Saheed El-Ali or Allah; he wanted them to know that they could not talk to him in just any kind of way. As he approached them, the phone of the commander rang. The Iraqi soldier looked at his phone's display and walked away to take the call in private.

"Hello, your Excellency," answered the soldier. "Yes, yes," he repeated. "It will be as you command, Your Excellency. I will take care of it. Consider it done."

The soldier called his men to him. They excused themselves from Abdul and walked over to the commander. They huddled together and whispered among themselves.

CHAPTER TWENTY-FOUR

Harry Graham paced the floor as he waited for the president. He was still angry about the way their first meeting ended, but he was more concerned about what he had learned earlier in the day. Michelle Mason was not lying. There is a movement in Kentucky designed to keep him from being re-elected. Everything she said was true. Republicans were finding someone to challenge him just so they could vote against him. There was plenty of time before the election to try to win back voters, but the Speaker knew his fate was tied to the president's. He had contemplated retirement but felt he had one term left in him. Besides, there was a big difference in leaving on your own terms and being forced out. He could not go out that way. Harry Graham wanted to reschedule this meeting. He wanted to send the other two Senators back to Washington, but he could not come up with a reasonable explanation.

The Senators from Ohio and Texas had joined him. None of them had legitimate reasons to dislike the new president. He was a Democrat, and that was reason enough. It was their job to give him a hard time. Senator Douglas Winston, of Ohio, resembled a modern-day Benjamin Franklin. He was bald and was always looking over the top of his wire-rimmed bifocals. His soft appearance, five-foot eight-inch pudgy body, and big feet gave people a first impression that he was a gentle, harmless intellectual. Senator Winston looked the part of a nerd, but he was heartless. He did not have a sense of humor, and he rarely smiled. This was due largely to a childhood of being bullied and ridiculed. He had been an accountant by trade and decided to get into politics for vindictive reasons. Senator Winston was chairman of the Judiciary Committee, which decides whether or not to proceed with impeachment.

Senator Richard Vincent, of Texas, was as arrogant and as dishonest as they come. His six-foot six-inch frame magnified his arrogance as he looked down on everyone. He served a couple of years in the army, more of a career move than a patriotic choice. His pride convinced him to wear contacts. He did not grow facial hair and he kept his military-style haircut. The senator had put on a few pounds over the years, but a few more would not hurt him. His stature and look gave him an intimidating appearance, and he loved it. Senator Vincent was by far the wealthiest person on Capitol Hill. He was born to wealthy parents in the oil business, and he had not encountered a problem that money could not resolve. Senator Vincent despised President Bush, both of them. If both of them could become president, surely he could as well. They were his motivation to pursue the White House and kicking out the current president would be an excellent start.

These were the men Harry Graham had formed an alliance with. The three of them were a formidable team, with a lot of power and quite a few people owing them favors. However, their biggest and most glaring weakness was self-survival. Neither of the three, and very few others on Capitol Hill, believed in taking one for the team. Harry Graham wanted to stay in office more than he wanted Patton out of office. His pacing was due more to his concern for himself, not his anger at the president. He wondered if it was too late. He had been identified in newspapers nationwide and had appeared on Michelle Mason's show as the main person leading the charge to impeach the president. How could he change that perception without showing his hand to Senators Winston and Vincent? One slip-up would make them suspicious.

Bobby Parker took two steps inside the room and slowly looked around. All three congressmen focused their attention on him. The Speaker was a bit startled as Bobby almost stepped into his path. He quickly regained his composure and put on his poker face. He knew the president had arrived. Bobby took another step inside the room and made sure he didn't miss anything. The room was easy to check because there were no bathrooms, closets, or any other room off of this one. With everything that had been going on lately, he was checking and double- checking everything that involved the president. Bobby made eye contact with each man. He did not like what he saw or felt. He could feel the contempt and stubbornness in each one. There was no physical threat present but if looks could kill, the president was in serious trouble.

After a couple of minutes, Bobby left the room. A few minutes later, Dale Patton walked in. He was met with polite greetings and firm handshakes from all. The Speaker introduced the two senators to the president. He emphasized Senator Winston's position on the Judiciary Committee. Harry Graham noticed something during the introduction of Senator Winston. It had appeared for a split-second and then was gone. Senator Winston was in awe of the president. Senator Winston had let his guard down for only a second, but the Speaker was sure of what he saw. If he noticed it, the president probably noticed it too. Maybe he could use this to his advantage.

"Let's hurry up and get this over with, gentlemen," said the President, "I have more important matters to attend to."

"Are any of those matters as important as keeping your job," asked Senator Vincent?

"Mr. Speaker, you better speak to your lap dog," said the president. "He will be back in Texas working on one of his daddy's oil wells before he realizes what happened if he thinks he can intimidate me."

"Dale Patton, you don't scare me."

"All right, calm down, Richard," ordered Graham. "We have work to do. Senator Winston, don't you have something to say to the President?"

"Yes, yes, of course," said Senator Winston. "Mr. President, a lot of people are calling for your head. They say you are on a power trip, insane, or grossly incompetent. I hope you have a good explanation for your actions, specifically for why you are bombing a country based on the actions of a handful or terrorists. As Chairman of the Judiciary Committee I am being pressured to initiate a formal inquiry into your actions."

"Senator, you mentioned that a lot of people were calling for my head. Everything that I have seen, read, or heard in the last couple of days indicates that the people approve of my actions. Any pressure you may be experiencing appears to be more of a nudge from your partners in crime like these other two here."

"Regardless of your opinion, Mr. President," said Senator Vincent, "the facts remain the same. You have ordered a military assault against a country with no proof of that country having done anything to justify your self-serving actions. On top of that, you have not been given approval to assault Iraq by Congress, the UN or NATO. You, sir, have some explaining to do."

"You, Senator Vincent, are very confused," said the president. Speaking of explanations, I hear that your company is under investigation for a laundry list of things, with the very least being tax evasion. Some very serious infractions are on that list. Maybe you would like to explain those things to us. It seems like we all are looking for explanations. The difference is, in a worst-case scenario, my prison cell would be similar to an executive lounge. You, on the other hand, would be forced to entertain your fellow inmates for a long, long time. Lord forbid if any of those inmates were people you have betrayed. I will decide who I can share confidential information with and when to share it, and you are the last person on earth I would share anything with. I don't have to explain anything to either of you, because I don't report to you individually, so don't come at me with veiled threats and intimidation. Yes, you can make things a little difficult for me, but believe me, I can make your lives miserable."

At that moment, Bobby came into the room. He walked over to the president and whispered something in his ear.

"I'll be out in just a minute," said Patton.

The three Senators were a bit stunned. They knew the President would be a tough foe, but they had never seen him retaliate in such a manner. He had just informed them that he was the president, with a lot of authority at his fingertips and not afraid to use it. They received the message loud and clear. They would not back down, but they would proceed with caution.

Senator Vincent appeared to be the most uncomfortable at that moment. He knew the majority of the president's comments were directed at him. He was taken back a bit, because he had just received notice that morning that his oil company was under investigation for a number of things, just as the president had said. Now he was wondering if the president had initiated the investigation. The story had not even appeared through any media outlet yet. Why was this news so important that the president would be informed of it in the middle of a terrorist situation? Maybe he knew about it before the terrorist hijacking. All kind of scenarios ran through his mind. Senator Vincent had shown his fangs too soon.

"It appears that duty calls," said Graham. "But know this, Mr. President: even you are not above the law. You know what the law requires in situations like this, and you have ignored those laws. We want you to know before you leave that we intend to file a proposal to start a formal inquiry to have you impeached."

"We," the President asked as he looked at Senator Winston? "For some reason your threat doesn't surprise me. On your way back to Washington, you should think this through very carefully. You, Senator Vincent, should practice thinking before speaking."

The President turned and headed for the door. The three of them watched in silence as the president left the room. Bobby and three other agents waited for the president to exit the room. They took their positions around him and began to walk up the corridor. As they approached the nearest exit, two other agents joined them.

"Are the senators behaving themselves," asked Bobby. "As quiet as it was when you came out, you must have put them in their place."

Patton smiled and said, "Remind me to thank Tommy for that bit of information concerning the investigation of Vincent Oil. It turned out to be very useful. What is this news that requires my immediate attention?"

"I have some good news for you," said Bobby. "It seems that Darrin has found that missing evidence he's been looking for. He says he has your proof that Iraq is involved in the hijacking of AWA Flight 454."

"That's the best news I have had since I've been in office. Those senators are lucky I didn't have that information beforehand. Let's go see what Darrin has. I knew he would come through. I am glad he figured it out before we hear from Ockbar again."

"Clermont, Duncan, General Phillips, and Tommy have been asked to meet you in the war room immediately so that they can be informed of Darrin's breakthrough. Darrin is waiting for your call."

"Good," said Patton, "maybe this will put everyone's mind at ease."

Patton, Bobby, and the rest of the president's protection continued on toward the war room. They kept a steady, continuous pace but were not in a hurry. Patton was relieved to hear of the proof of Iraq's involvement, even though he had not seen it. He completely trusted Darrin; his work had always been well researched and accurate. However, he prayed that he would not have to make good on his threat against Iraq. He wasn't getting cold feet, and he did think the killing of innocent lives required a strong retaliation. He had hoped the destruction of Karbala would be enough. That was his warning shot, and he hoped it wouldn't be ignored. Like any good soldier, the President was well aware of what was at stake; he was never anxious to fight, but he had never been scared to fight, either.

The president and his security approached the war room. Patton and Bobby went inside, as the Secret Service took their places outside the room. Duncan, Clermont, General Phillips, and Tommy were all waiting for them when they arrived. They were more anxious than the president to see Darrin's proof.

"How did the meeting go with Graham and his wanna-be's?" asked Clermont?

"It went as expected. They are trying to impose their will over me through scare tactics and intimidation. As soon as this hostage situation has been resolved, they will get more of my attention than they want. Are there any new developments that should be brought to my attention before I contact Darrin?"

"There is one thing you should know," said Tommy.

"Let's hear it."

"The two rogue CIA agents, John Conklin and Bruce McAllister, were apprehended about thirty minutes ago in New York. They should be in Washington in the next couple of hours."

"That's good news. Where were they?"

"They were at the JFK Airport with false passports and tickets to Germany."

"They were together?"

"Yes sir, which wasn't very smart on their part."

"What about Marty Hickman? What's the scoop on him?"

"Nothing on him yet, sir, but the FBI believe he is still in the city or close by."

"I see. Is there anything else I should know?"

When no one else spoke up, the president picked up the phone at his station and dialed the vice president. Now he understood why Bobby continued to use extra security, just in case Marty Hickman wanted to finish the job that Dooley and Pitts had started. The president reached Darrin after a couple of rings. They spoke for just a minute or two before the President ended the connection.

"Bobby, dial up the vice president's cam and put it on the big screen. Darrin is going to be on in a minute and show us what he has."

"As you wish, sir," said Bobby.

Bobby did as instructed, and the big flat-screen converted into a big laptop. They were tuned in and waiting on the vice president. They didn't have to wait long.

"Hello, gentlemen," said the vice president. "I hope I didn't keep you waiting too long?"

"Not at all," said the president. "We just got here. What do you have for us?"

"Well, Mr. President, you know that I have been watching the two terrorist productions over and over, trying to figure out what I was missing. There was something eerily familiar about them that I couldn't put my finger on. Then Tommy said something to me that made a lot of sense. He suggested that I look for Iraq in the films and stop looking at the terrorists. So, I stopped thinking terrorist and started thinking Iraq, since that's the connection we're trying to prove. Then it came to me. Then I saw how Iraq is involved. Let me show you what I am talking about."

Darrin placed a snapshot of the two current hostage assassinations on the screen. The first was a snapshot of the little old lady who was the victim in the first production. The second snapshot was of the four Americans that were in the second production.

"I am going to put a couple more snapshots up, but before I do, take a good look at these two," said Darrin.

Darrin waited a minute before putting up the third snapshot. It too looked to be a hostage situation in which a man was about to be shot.

"Do you see anything these three photos have in common?" asked Darrin.

"Yes," said General Phillips, 'the terrorists in the third photo are in the same positions around the hostage as those in the first two."

"Exactly," said Darrin. "Now let me show you the fourth photo."

Again, the terrorists were in the same positions around two more men who were about to be killed.

"Now watch this," said Darrin.

The vice president clicked a button, and the terrorists in the third and fourth photos were wearing Iraqi military uniforms. They were Iraqi soldiers.

"Photo number three," explained Darrin, "is a 1993 file photo of Iraqi soldiers dealing with an American businessman whom the country alleged was an American spy. Photo number four is another file photo of Iraqi soldiers dealing with two alleged Iranian spies. Needless to say, the fate of those three men was the same as the fate of our citizens who were killed in the first two photos."

"You're implying that the terrorists who killed our citizens are actually Iraqi soldiers?" asked the president?

"I am doing more than implying, Mr. President. I am stating for a fact that they are Iraqi soldiers. The film was tampered with to cover up their uniforms. If you look really closely, you can see different bulges in their clothes, which correspond to the location of different patches and medals on their uniform."

"That's some good information," said the president, "and I'll take it, but it's not as concrete as I had hoped."

"Hold on a second, Mr. President. I'm not finished. Let me show you a couple more photographs. Take a look at this first guy who took out the little old lady."

Darrin had enlarged the face of the terrorist that killed the little old lady and placed it on the screen. He then placed a photo of an Iraqi military platoon in full uniform on the screen, with the face of one soldier circled. He enlarged the face of that soldier also.

"These two people are the same person," said Darrin. "We have a positive match. We don't know his name. He was just an infantryman in that platoon photo. Our intelligence team couldn't find anything else on him."

"That's all we need," said the president. "You can't get better than positive identification. Good job, Darrin."

"Thank you, Mr. President, but I have more news that is probably not as favorable."

"Spill it, Darrin, what's going on?"

"We have received another production from the terrorist. It has already been downloaded and forwarded to Camp David. I expect it will be delivered to you at any moment."

"Have you seen it?"

"No one has seen it yet. I have left instructions to be informed once it has been delivered to you. I plan to look at it at about the same time that you are viewing it."

As if on cue, Bobby pressed his right hand to his ear. He then left the room for a brief moment and returns with a small package in his hand. He took it directly to the president and hands it to him.

"I believe it has just arrived," said the president. "Again, I want to say thank you and good work."

"Thank you, sir, but a lot of credit goes to Tommy. He put me on the right track."

"Tommy is sitting right here. Thanks to both of you. I'll talk to you soon."

Darrin's transmission ended, and the screen went black. Bobby disconnected from the cam feed and then turned the television off. The President examined the small package. He removed the case containing the disc.

"Duncan, General, are our forces and allies ready and informed?"

"They are," answered Duncan.

"Sir, the only thing keeping them at bay is that they haven't received your command to proceed," said General Phillips.

"And the recovery team is aware that they only have a small window in which to take out Ockbar Shalam and his men and bring the captives home?"

"They are looking forward to the challenge, Mr. President," said Duncan.

"In that case, let's get the show on the road. Bobby, put this in the player. Let's find out which path Ockbar is forcing me to take."

Bobby took the case and walked over to the wall that contained the large flat-screen television. He opened the case, removed the disc, and pressed a button on the player. When the holder came out, Bobby placed the disc inside and then pressed the same button again to close it. He pressed the Play button and then picked up the remote and headed back to his station. As he passed the President, Bobby placed the remote down on the table in front of him and went back to his station.

The tape started with a close-up of Ockbar.

"Hello Mr. President," Ockbar said. "I have one final production for you. I hope you slept well last night because I didn't. There were a lot of fireworks going off close by that kept me awake. Since I was awake anyway, I decided to make good use of my time. I hope you appreciate my latest production. I think it is my finest work. It seems that you have ignored my other messages and the urgency I have been trying to portray. Therefore, I am convinced that if this production does not convince you of the seriousness of the matter, nothing will. I will then kill the remaining passengers and look for other creative ways to get your attention. From this moment on, you will realize that Ockbar Shalam is not someone you can ignore. Enjoy the show."

The camera panned over to a similar scene. There were a group of hostages surrounded by terrorists, and one was holding a nine-millimeter Glock pistol. The hijacked plane could be seen in the background, with a bunch of crying passengers looking out the windows. A couple of terrorists were walking among the passengers on the plane. The big difference between this production and the others was that the hostages who were about to be assassinated were all children.

Ockbar had gotten the president's attention. His eyes were almost slits, and his jaws tightened as he clenched his teeth. The president wasn't the only one in the room who had a reaction to seeing children seconds away from assassination. Everyone in the room reacted in some way. Bobby, similar to the president, revealed his concern only on his face. The others showed their disapproval with facial expressions and verbal comments. Phrases like "son-of-a-bitch", "Oh God no. Please! God, no!" and "Not the kids, please don't hurt the kids" were spoken by the others. Tommy's eyes started to fill with water.

The lens of the camera zoomed in on the main event. The gunman in the midst of the children raised his weapon chest high and pulled back the hammer. He pointed it in the direction of the little girl on the left-hand side of the screen. The gunman pulled the trigger. The echo of the gunshot seemed to last forever. The children all let out blood-curdling screams and cried even louder. It was impossible for them to cry any harder. Everyone in the war room flinched. It was as if they were in denial and could not believe the gunman pulled the trigger. Tommy and Clermont turned their faces from the television for a brief moment. They could not bear to watch. The others were confused until reality set in. The reality was that none of the children were hurt; they were scared out of their mind, but not hurt. The terrorist that had been to the right of the little girl now lay dead, with blood streaming from his chest. He had suffered a gunshot wound to the heart.

A few seconds later, one of the terrorists on the plane pulled his pistol and shot one of the other terrorists. A couple more flashes of gunfire were seen. The passengers ducked and screamed in fear as two dead terrorists lay on the floor of the plane. Ockbar took a couple of steps forward to see what was happening. Simultaneously, a separate terrorist came from out of nowhere and shot Ockbar in the back of the head, while the gunman standing near the children quickly turned and shot one of the other terrorists nearby. The exiting bullet caused Ockbar's forehead to explode, as blood, bone, and brain matter sprayed fifty feet. As Ockbar fell, face first to the floor of the hangar, the assassin redirected his aim to the camera operator and shot him.

Abdul hung onto the camera as long as he could before collapsing to the floor. This caused the camera to point up at the ceiling. Patton, Clermont, and the rest of the war room crew became very uneasy as they looked at the filming of the ceiling for about thirty seconds before the camera was refocused.

The camera was slowly reset to its previous position. The children were still huddled together, crying. Ockbar's body and the corpses of the other terrorists could be seen lying on the floor. The passengers on the plane were slowly rising back up and peeking out the window to see whatever they could. Finally, the terrorist who had shot Ockbar stepped in front of the camera.

"Greetings President Patton," said Ockbar's assassin. "I bring you a message from Prime Minister Saheed el-Ali. The prime minister changed his mind about helping the US hostages. He decided that aiding our people is more important than hating yours. As you have witnessed, the entire cell that was responsible for this atrocity has been eliminated. The prime minister expects your military forces and those of your allies to immediately vacate our land and our skies. In return, the remaining survivors will be flown to the Cairo International Airport, where you can make arrangements to have them safely returned to their homeland. The prime minister would also like you to know he will not forget the destruction you brought to Karbala."

The assassin walked away from the camera toward the children. He tried to calm them down as he guided them back onto the plane. The camera stayed on another two minutes before it went black.

"I can't believe it," said Duncan. "It's over. They folded and threw in their hand. We did it, Mr. President, and none of the children were hurt."

"At least not physically," said Tommy, "but they will have some lifetime emotional scars."

"What exactly did we do?" asked the president? "Six innocent people are dead, a Secret Service Agent is fighting for his life, and an entire city in Iraq is in ruins. I'm not even counting the five terrorists that were killed. I have no pity for them, but what did we really win? Yes, we kept more people from being killed, but the big question is, have we convinced the world that the United States will no longer engage in lengthy conversation when our people and our nation are threatened?"

"I think that message has been very convincingly delivered," said Tommy.

"John, contact the Iraqi prime minister and thank him for his assistance. Inform him that all military presence will remain until the remaining passengers have been returned unharmed. Remind him that he is still under the same twenty-four hour mandate, and my watch indicates he has a little less than twenty hours remaining. Tell the prime minister that I want all of our dead to be properly prepared and dressed for a proper funeral. I want them placed in nice caskets and put on the plane. I also want Ockbar's and Rahman's bodies on board. The caskets should be on the same plane as the passengers."

"I'm on it," said Clermont as he got up and left the room.

"General Phillips and Duncan, you two contact our military leaders and allies and update them on the situation. Inform them that all systems are go if AWA Flight 454 has not landed in Cairo in the previously allotted time frame. However, have them check with you one last time before they proceed. When that plane begins its journey home, I want our Air Force to escort it back to the States."

"As you wish Mr. President," said General Phillips as he and Duncan left the room.

"Tommy, I want you to contact Darrin. He has probably looked at the video by now and is aware of what has happened. I want you and him to contact NATO, the UN, and the heads of state of the allies that backed us in this situation. Bring them up to date on what has happened and send them the proof we have of Iraq's involvement. Ask them to send us their documented statements that this was an act of war by Iraq, and they approve of the action we took."

"What about Harry Graham and his watch dogs?"

"What about them?"

"Don't you want to bring them up to date on everything that has happened in the last few hours?"

"No, I don't," said Patton. "As a matter of fact, I want as much of this kept from them as possible. If I know that they are wasting their time on trying to impeach me, I can relax for a little while and concentrate on other things. I want you to give the entire story to that Channel 8 anchor, Michelle Mason. She helped us out a bit, whether she intended to or not. Give her an exclusive. After she breaks the news, schedule a press conference and confirm her story."

"She will love that, and the senators will be boiling."

"Be sure that she knows that the Speaker of the House and his crew are not aware of this information just yet. Tell her to feel free to use that information as she chooses."

"You don't believe in taking prisoners, do you sir?" asked Tommy"

"Not anymore," said Patton. "The last prisoner I took killed one of my men. Let's get to work."

"Yes sir," said Tommy as he too left the room.

"Well, Bobby, hopefully tonight will be the last night I will have to spend here for a while."

"That would be fine with me, Mr. President."

Bobby left the room, with the president close behind him. The two guards outside the door fell in behind them as soon as the president cleared the doorway. Two other guards filed in on each side of the president as they turned the corner.

CHAPTER TWENTY-FIVE

Michelle Mason sat at her station, anxiously waiting for the cue that indicated live broadcasting. Trying to maintain her professional demeanor, while not showing too much enthusiasm, she was excited, yet surprised, to receive this exclusive from the White House. Her first and second meetings with the first lady were not ideal. Such confrontations have prevented previous news anchors from ever receiving clearance to step foot in the White House, except for a visitor's tour. In a few seconds, she would interrupt regular broadcasting to announce that she would be delivering information very few people knew about outside of the President's inner circle. There was her cue.

"Good evening, ladies and gentlemen, this is Michelle Mason, interrupting your regularly scheduled program to bring you a Channel 8 exclusive. Highly sought-after terrorist Ockbar Shalam has been killed, and the passengers and crew of AWA Flight 454 are on their way home. Channel 8's News at Six starts in fifteen minutes. Stay tuned for the coverage that only Channel 8 can bring you."

Patton was back in his suite, watching the broadcast. He was joined by Bobby and Tommy. Katie had just left for Washington. Tommy was still a little excited but was getting used to being part of the inner circle. He didn't want to appear too comfortable, but he didn't want to appear to be too stiff, either. As nice as this was, it was still business. This was evident every time he looked at Bobby, who seldom sat down and seemed to always be on his guard.

"I imagine Ms. Mason was surprised to hear from you," said Patton?

"Surprised isn't the word, "replied Tommy. "She was ecstatic. At first, she was a bit defensive and thought I was trying to manipulate her in some way. I convinced her differently, and she could barely contain her excitement. Then she kept thanking me over and over again and asking why her."

"What did you tell her?"

"I didn't give her a reason. I told her I could call the Channel 15 anchor if she wasn't interested. She apologized, begged me not to hang up, and assured me that she was indeed interested."

"Indeed," Bobby said sarcastically. "She is probably as excited as Harry Graham is pissed."

"You know he's hot," said Patton. "Wait until he hears about proof of Iraq's involvement and the signed documents we have from the U.N. and N.A.T.O. I wish I could see his face at that moment."

"When he hears the news, it might be wise to have medical technicians close by," said Tommy. "By the way Mr. President, Ms. Mason will be reporting on a breaking story just for you."

"What are you talking about, Tommy?"

"It seems that Channel 8 has had people investigating Vincent Oil for a while now. They have found some less than legal dealings, which she will air right after the hijacking story."

"The two stories don't go together. Why now?"

"She heard about Senators Graham, Winston, and Vincent trying to give you a hard time, so she is going to tie it in with the hijacking story. They were going to wait until ratings week, but this is her way of thanking you for the exclusive. She is also going to touch on the Speaker's unlikely chances of being re-elected. She doesn't have anything on Senator Winston yet, but plans to follow up on a rumor regarding financial impropriety."

"I must say that I like the way she shows her gratitude. I'm afraid to talk too loudly. She has ears everywhere."

"How is she going to tie those stories together," asked Bobby

"She's going to spin it like it's a political power struggle; the good political servants versus the corrupt political hacks. Of course, you, Mr. President, will be the good guy trying to do his job, while the bad guys try to derail and discredit you by throwing everything they can at you. After she identifies Senators Graham, Winston, and Vincent as the bad guys, she will go into those other stories that I just mentioned."

"It sounds like she is running your adversaries out of Washington for you," said Bobby.

"I wish I would have known: I would have given her a list of names."

They enjoy a laugh as the Channel 8 News came back on the air. Patton picked up the remote and turned off the television. Bobby and Tommy turned to look at the President with surprise. He opened the drawer of a nearby end-table, took out a deck of cards, and began to remove the cards from the pack.

"Don't look at me like I've lost my mind," Patton said, smiling. "We all know what Ms. Mason is about to say. After all, we gave her the story. Who's interested in a game of poker?"

"Count me in," Tommy said, laughing.

"I don't mind teaching the new guy a few things," said Bobby. "You really do need to learn how to bluff, Dale."

All three shared a good laugh as they followed Patton into the kitchen. The president put his hand in his pocket and pulled out a coin. "Hey Tommy, catch," said Patton as he flipped him the coin.

Tommy reacted just in time to catch the coin. He looked at it and couldn't believe his eyes. He brought the coin up closer to his face and looked at it on both sides. He had just caught an Indian-head nickel; a buffalo on one side and the head of an Indian on the other. It took all he could do to keep his emotions in check; he had just been initiated into the group.

"Thanks Dale," he finally said, "this is the best thing anyone has ever given me."

"I know you have never fought in any military battles, but you have been a real soldier the last few days. I would go into battle with you anytime."

"Okay, let's play cards," Tommy said, "before I have to go find a hankie. I better put this away. You may want to borrow it back before the night is over."

"Bobby, if Tommy wins shoot, him."

Bobby looked Tommy directly in the eyes and said, "My pleasure, Mr. President!"

Laughing hard, they each pulled out a chair and took a seat at the kitchen table. Bobby manages to stop laughing long enough to say something into his headset, then he removed his sunglasses and placed them on the table.

Tommy was in seventh heaven. He couldn't keep the smile off of his face. What a difference an international crisis and a few days could make. Patton shuffled the deck of cards and placed them on the table. Bobby cut the cards, Patton picked them back up, and then the president started dealing. All the smiles had vanished.

CHAPTER TWENTY-SIX

Katherine's funeral was beautiful. It was broadcast nationally and received very high ratings, especially for Channel 8 out of DC. Michelle Mason made sure Katherine's heroic exploits were well known. Though Mason's reasons for widely communicating Katherine's heroic deeds were partly out of gratitude for the exclusive, she also felt guilty for breaking the story too soon. Michelle believed that her over aggressive desire to break the big story had put Katherine's life in danger. Her efforts to rectify this situation were commendable.

Ruth Wilcox, along with everyone else on AWA Flight 454, was eager to sing Katherine's praises. They could not say enough good things about her. Every one of them attended Katherine's funeral; they each placed a red rose on her casket. A photo of Ruth placing the last of over two-hundred roses on Katherine's casket was the cover of the February issue of Time magazine.

Michelle Mason, along with other media sources, made sure that Katherine's story circled the globe. Katherine Morrison became the icon for strong, spiritual, caring women. The White House was inundated with mail addressed to Katie, praising her mother and wishing her family the best of everything.

Katherine's story was on the cover of every major news magazine, and she was to posthumously receive the Presidential Medal of Freedom and the Congressional Gold Medal. They are the two highest civilian medals that the United States awards. While the president awards the Medal of Freedom, the Congressional Gold Medal is presented through an act of Congress. It was no big secret that the successful vote on the Congressional Gold Medal for Katherine was Congress's way of apologizing. They had been the recipient of more than a few unfavorable articles because they had not supported the president's actions during the hijacking situation.

WILLIAM I. BRAZLEY JR.

Enhanced DNA Publishing
DenolaBurton@EnhancedDNA1.com
www.EnhancedDNAPublishing.com

BEWARE THE POTUS

www.ingramcontent.com/pod-product-compliance
Lightning Source LLC
Chambersburg PA
CBHW021033130626
46552CB00005B/1814